Murderous Cruise Habit

Dawn Brookes
Large Print Edition

Murderous Cruise Habit

A Rachel Prince Mystery

Dawn Brookes

Oakwood Publishing

To Barbara and all the nuns at Chigwell

Chapter 1

Rachel had barely finished unpacking when she received a visit from the chief of security, Jack Waverley. The chief was a man Rachel considered a friend, even if he did occasionally resent her involvement in investigating crimes committed on board the Coral Queen. She doubted his visit so early on boarding day would be one that came under the banner of friendship.

She was right. Following the preliminary niceties and greetings, the chief came to the point of his visit.

"I have an unusual request," he said, coughing. The cough was something he always did when embarrassed or when sharing sensitive information. "Erm, I realise it's a bit of an imposition, and you and your family are on holiday."

Rachel wondered what would be coming next. Her parents were with her for a Caribbean cruise, along with her close friend, Lady Marjorie Snellthorpe.

"Perhaps you should just tell me what this is all about, Chief." She was beginning to think he would never get to the point, well aware he could prevaricate at times.

"Well, erm, I'm asking on behalf of Captain Jenson, really. You see, the deputy captain has gone down with a case of laryngitis. He would normally take the Sunday ceremony. Tomorrow's service is being held in the Coral Theatre rather than the chapel, as we anticipate a large number of religious people will be attending." He coughed again before Rachel got around to asking him what he meant by that last sentence. "Although the deputy's in work as usual, no-one would be able to hear him. Best type of service, if you ask me." He chuckled at his own joke.

Rachel smiled politely. "I take it you're asking if my father will stand in for the deputy. Is that right?"

"Captain Jenson would be most grateful if he would. I'm the next in line, but it really isn't my thing." His pleading eyes had already won her over, but she paused for a suitable length of time to increase his discomfort before answering.

"Let's ask. I'm sure my father won't mind, but I can't speak for him."

Waverley's relief was palpable.

They went to meet Rachel's parents in the adjacent suite so that the chief could deliver the unusual request. After introductions and another round of friendly formality, Rachel encouraged

Waverley to tell her father the reason for his presence. The chief explained his predicament, much to the amusement of Rachel watching on. If he'd expected her to do it for him, he was mistaken. The only thing missing was Marjorie, who would have thoroughly enjoyed his discomfort.

"I would be happy to oblige. I'm always up for a challenge," Brendan Prince answered. "I will need to know if there are any special dos and don'ts so I don't offend anyone."

"I'll send a second officer over to brief you, as one of them generally does a reading during the service. The only thing I know for certain is that you end with the sailor's hymn. It's, erm, tradition to do so." Waverley coughed again. "I'm afraid I don't attend the services, but even I know that hymn."

Rachel's father nodded in understanding. "I think I can do that. I look forward to meeting the second officer you mentioned. Does he or she have a name?"

"Gareth Butler. I'll ask him to stop by later this evening. Thank you. Oh, there is one more thing. There's a party of nuns on board; I assume they'll attend. They wanted to take over the chapel for a mass, but we don't allow that."

Rachel raised her eyebrows. "I thought nuns took a vow of poverty."

"Nuns, like vicars, need a break occasionally, Rachel," her father chided.

"Quite," said Waverley. "I won't take up any more of your time, Mr and Mrs Prince, or yours, Rachel."

"It was good to meet you, Chief," said Rachel's mother, Susan.

After Waverley left, Rachel asked about the sailor's hymn and her father explained that singing it was one of the many superstitions sailors held.

"Even the most hardened sailor realises that the power of the sea is not under their control."

Rachel sat at the back of the Coral Theatre with Marjorie on her left and her mother on her right. She felt anticipation and pride as she waited for the interdenominational Sunday service to begin, pleased her father had accepted the invitation to conduct the service.

Rachel watched people of all ages and nationalities entering to join the congregation as the theatre filled up. Waverley had been right; attendance was unusually high.

"It's like the United Nations," remarked Marjorie, leaning forwards so that Susan Prince could hear what she was saying.

"It's wonderful, isn't it? I noticed the same thing on a smaller scale when I attended a service in the chapel on a previous cruise," Rachel replied. "I met a woman who devoured rich men and then spat them out again after she'd fleeced them. She was hoping to hitch up with the captain."

"Oh, I do like the sound of her," said Marjorie with a twinkle in her eye.

"And here comes the religious order the chief mentioned last night," said Susan.

Rachel and Marjorie swivelled their heads to the right as a mass of blue filled the upper stairway. Around thirty nuns walked slowly down the central staircase with another few going down the steps of the far aisle. They made their way to the front rows of the auditorium and filled the seats there.

"Why the silence, do you imagine?" asked Marjorie.

"I don't know," answered Rachel. "Perhaps they've taken a vow of silence for the duration of the service. They're younger than I expected."

"And exceptionally pretty, from the faces I can see. That's unusual," remarked Susan.

"Oh, Mum! You're not suggesting nuns have to be ugly, are you?"

"Not at all! But I would expect some variation in height, weight and looks amongst such a large group, wouldn't you?"

"Your mother's right there," interjected Marjorie. "The only difference among them is skin colour, from what little I can see of the gathering. Other than that, they are all roughly the same shape, and their faces, those I can see, are rather beautiful. It does seem odd, almost like an unnatural selection."

"Well here come the older ones," whispered Rachel.

Five mature looking nuns wearing dark grey habits as opposed to the royal blue of the younger women walked reverently down the steps to join the others at the front. The holy order had become a focus of interest among others in the auditorium. Hushed conversations and inquisitive looks followed the women to their seats. Apart from a little jostling noise at the entrance, the nuns entered silently. They remained silent even when seated, as far as Rachel could make out from the back. It was peculiar.

"Look, there's Sarah." Marjorie nudged Rachel away from her musings and she followed the direction of the elderly woman's gaze to where a small group of ship's officers had entered via the stage doors, taking seats next to the nuns on the front row.

"That's the first time I've seen her in uniform other than in a photograph," remarked Susan. "You're absolutely right, Rachel, she looks gorgeous in her pristine whites. Have you heard from her since we boarded yesterday?"

Sarah had been Rachel's best friend since their school days and was well-known to her parents, as she had grown up in the village where Rachel's father was a vicar.

"Just a quick call last night to say welcome aboard and that she's looking forward to catching up with us all sometime today. She's on call until tonight."

The theatre quietened as Rachel's father strolled towards the lectern. He was dressed in a grey suit, but wore his clerical collar. He welcomed the international congregation and briefly explained what would happen during the service.

"Please refer to the Order of Service and the hymn sheets, as these will help you follow along. Feel free to join in with the hymns and prayers. If you are able, please stand to sing the hymns; otherwise, remain seated."

Rachel had been brought up under the care of Brendan Prince as a father and his spiritual tutelage as vicar. He was an amicable man, well able to put people at ease, and he conducted the service with his usual grace, humour and aplomb. Rachel couldn't have been more proud. It was lovely to have her parents with her for this, their first cruise, along with Marjorie, a sprightly octogenarian who put many of her peers to shame. Rachel had met Marjorie during her first ever voyage, and they became firm friends following that meeting.

The only person missing from her party was Carlos, Rachel's fiancé, who was in Italy attending a family funeral. She had offered to go with him, but he'd gallantly declined, as her parents had been looking forward to the cruise holiday and getting to meet all the crew members she had got to know through Sarah. Her parents rarely took holidays, so they were also keen to experience the activities available on board her beloved cruise ship.

"Why you like going on cruises anyway when all you come across is murder and mayhem, I'll never know," Carlos had teased her.

"I don't think I can answer that question and appear sane," she had retorted.

"Besides, your parents and Marjorie want to celebrate your new job, and I won't deprive them of that."

Rachel had passed her sergeant's exams in the autumn and been offered a job as a detective sergeant. The job would involve a move to Leicester, so she would be leaving London after the voyage. She'd loved living in London, where she rented a flat owned by Marjorie, but the new job was an opportunity she couldn't turn down.

Leicester was the city where she had solved her first crime whilst spending the summer there working on her dissertation. After the remains of King Richard III were discovered under a car park in Leicester, the subject matter for a keen history student had been obvious. This occurred long before she'd thought about joining the police force. That particular crime was something she had completely forgotten about until it was all brought back to her when she sent away her application form and attended an interview. She was surprised to learn that DCI Molly Bond – the woman she had crossed paths with previously and who she had imagined would be opposed to working with her – was in favour of her appointment. Perhaps she was looking forward to putting Rachel in her place.

"Do you think she's taken me on to make my life difficult?" she had asked Carlos.

He had stared deeply into her eyes and spoken solemnly. "Whatever her reason, darling, she will soon find out that you are an investigative genius and Leicester will be lucky to have you. Anyway, if you don't like it, come and work with me. We could go into partnership. Or there's always the *Coral Queen*."

They had laughed together, knowing
that Jack Waverley would gladly give her
a job as a security officer on board the
Coral, having offered her a position each
time she sailed.

Her mother nudged her out of her
reverie to stand for the final hymn. Rachel
mouthed an apology. They sang the
sailor's hymn, *Eternal Father, Strong to
Save*, the words of the song pleading for
God's protection for all those at sea.
Rachel agreed it was particularly poignant
as she returned to the present.

With the service over, people were
quick to vacate their seats, hurrying
towards the exits to go on to their next
activity. Rachel was chatting to her
mother while Marjorie spoke to a man to
her left when a primal scream from the
front rows rang through the theatre.

Rachel looked downwards to see a
hubbub centring on the young nuns. She

could just make out her father, Sarah and
a few others attending to one of them on
the third row, but it was difficult to see
what was happening. Gasps and shouts
verging on hysteria came from the group
who up until that point had remained
silent.

An officer took to the stage.

"Please vacate the theatre as quickly as
possible. Our ship's nurse and members
of the crew are attending to a passenger
who has been taken ill. There's no need
for alarm; the ship's doctor is on his way.
Please clear the entrances as soon as
possible and continue with your holiday.
Enjoy the rest of your day and take
advantage of the activities and facilities
aboard our luxurious vessel."

Rachel's father made the sign of the
cross over the woman, who had now been
moved into the aisle, which didn't
convince her that all was well. She

noticed Dr Bentley, the chief medical officer whom she had met on previous cruises, arrive and take charge.

Marjorie cast a knowing look towards Rachel and she immediately realised the woman was dead. Just when she thought things couldn't get any worse, a loud wail erupted from the other side of Marjorie.

Chapter 2

Marjorie ushered the couple next to her towards the end of the row while Rachel and her mother moved to occupy the seats in front. The woman appeared to be in her mid-fifties, wearing a copper-red wig of long wavy hair that contrasted with her dark skin. She wore immaculately applied bright red lipstick. Her lips trembled as tears flowed down her cheeks and she looked at the man next to her.

"I know it's her, Connor. I just know."

The man with the distressed woman held her hand and put his arm around her. Rachel wasn't sure if he was her son. He was early thirties, dressed in knee-length khaki shorts and a white vest revealing muscular biceps. His skin tone was lighter than the woman's. He had short, tightly curled black hair.

"You can't think that, Gloria." The whites of his eyes became saucers as he looked helplessly towards Marjorie.

"Now, now, my dear, my name is Marjorie. Please tell us what is worrying you and we'll try to help."

The soothing tone of Marjorie's practical voice had the desired effect, and the woman stopped snivelling, sniffed in a deep breath and looked across at her.

"My daughter. I think that's my daughter down there. It looks bad."

The revelation shocked Rachel. The condition of the woman below appeared to be worse than bad.

"Would you like me to find out?" she asked.

"No, not at the moment."

Marjorie and Rachel exchanged quizzical glances while Susan spoke.

"But wouldn't it put your mind at ease?"

"No. I mean yes, but she can't know I'm here. She'll never speak to me again if she thinks I followed her. Our relationship is not as good as it should be. Anyway, I'm sure she's just fainted." The woman raised her head and looked hopefully at Marjorie while avoiding looking at the scene to the front of the theatre.

Rachel glanced down to where the medical team was attempting to resuscitate the young woman and knew it was far worse than a faint, but there was nothing anyone could do for the moment other than let the medics get on with their work.

"Perhaps you would like to tell us about it. Gloria, was it? These are my friends,

Rachel and Susan – the daughter and wife of the vicar who took the service."

"Yes, I'm Gloria. This is Connor, my husband." Gloria gestured to the man on her right. The three women disguised their surprise well as Marjorie continued.

"It helps to talk. If that is your daughter down there, why would she be upset to find you on the same cruise?"

"She doesn't like—"

"Me," interrupted Connor. "She thinks I married her mother for her money because there's an age difference. Not that you'd know it, looking at my beautiful wife here."

A flicker of a smile crossed Gloria's lips. "It's not only that. It's just she became troubled when my first marriage broke up. She adored her father."

"Adored? Past tense. Does that mean he's no longer with us?" asked Marjorie.

"It does mean that. The man was a no-good drunk – drank himself to death, but in her daughter's eyes, he was a saint." Connor spat the words out.

Rachel tried to sum him up as he spoke, pleased Marjorie was taking the lead so she could observe. He seemed genuinely concerned for his wife, but why the bitter tone? There were a good twenty years between them, if not more. He struck her as someone with a past, but she couldn't think why she felt that way.

"Connor's right. She always held her father on a pedestal. No-one could live up to the great man she wanted him to be, not even him." Gloria blew her nose and paused. "I think that's why she's becoming a nun, just to spite me. She left home at eighteen and went to live with her father. I think he was a disappointment to her, but she would never admit to that. He drank and she got in with the wrong people. She had money – I'm wealthy, you see. I gave her a generous allowance."

"Not that she appreciated it, from what I hear," interrupted Connor.

"People took advantage of her. The people who called themselves her friends were parasites. Even her father borrowed off her to buy expensive suits and throw lavish parties."

"All on Gloria's money," Connor said.

A theme was developing here and Rachel wondered if it was a case of like mother, like daughter when it came to buying affection.

Gloria continued, "When her father died, she went to pieces. Her so-called friends dropped her after I reduced her allowance. She worked for a few years in a school before leaving that job. These religious people appeared just at the right time for her. Now she's turned her back on me and joined them. She signed her allowance over to them, and as much as I resent it, I go along with it. I don't want to give her any excuse to hate me even more than she already does. In her head, I'm responsible for everything that has gone wrong in her life, while her father was responsible for everything good."

"Hate is a strong word," said Marjorie. "Your daughter still needs you and most likely loves you. I expect she has just lost sight of that in her grief and anger."

Gloria looked hopeful. "Do you think so? I do pray that's the case. I only came on this cruise to see what attraction this holy order holds for her, and to find out if she's genuinely happy or whether it's just another phase. If she is happy, I can take the pain of losing her. I mean, who can compete with God, eh?" A weak smile followed.

Rachel noticed that the woman below was being moved on to a stretcher with two women in grey following the medical team and Chief Waverley out of the theatre.

"Are you sure you don't want us to find out if that's your daughter down there?" asked Marjorie.

"Perhaps you could ask your husband?" Gloria looked towards Susan. "We are in room 7262. I would be extremely grateful."

"Of course I will. May I ask your surname?"

"Franks," answered Connor. "Gloria's daughter's name is Jacintha Balch. Balch was her father's surname."

"Sir, ladies, I'm going to have to ask you to leave the theatre. We have a talk starting in ten minutes." Rachel saw one of the crew standing next to Gloria. How long had he been there?

"Of course. We were just about to leave anyway," answered Marjorie.

Gloria and Connor left immediately, while Rachel and Marjorie waited for Susan to retrieve her things from where she had been sitting before they joined the couple.

"I was convinced he was her son," Susan said.

"Yes, he's got to be a few decades younger. She appears refined, but he strikes me as a bit of an actor. His posh American accent seems forced."

"A gigolo, perhaps," said Marjorie. "I wonder if the daughter is right about him."

"Being a gold digger, you mean? Oh yes, I'm sure that's exactly what he is."

"Rachel! You can't say that, you've only just met the man," her mother said, exasperated. "He seemed devoted to her, and protective."

"Of her money, yes. Mum, I'll apologise if I'm wrong, but hey – what's any of it to do with us anyway?"

Other than a motive for murder.

Rachel kept that last thought to herself.

Chapter 3

Rachel didn't appreciate being hustled out of the theatre; it was frustrating. She would have liked more time to speak with the Franks couple as they had piqued her interest.

"Don't worry, we'll find out from your father later on what happened. I take it he's still down there somewhere?" Marjorie took her arm and led her towards the nearest coffee lounge. Rachel's mother followed anxiously.

"I do hope the poor young woman is all right and that she's not Gloria's daughter. Gloria seemed such a nice woman. I couldn't see what was happening down the front because I still had my reading glasses on."

Breaking bad news to Susan wasn't something either woman wanted to do, so Rachel and Marjorie kept quiet.

"I think tea is in order," said Marjorie, calling over one of the waiters. "It's been quite a start to the day." Marjorie was a great believer in the English conviction that tea could cure all ills.

"Oh yes, that would be good. Do you mind ordering for me? I need to go to the ladies."

As soon as her mother was out of earshot, Rachel turned to Marjorie. "Please tell me this isn't foul play. I don't think my parents could stand it. Poor Dad; first he has to conduct a service while he's on holiday, and now this – whatever this is."

"Do your parents know about the murders on your previous cruises?"

"Only the first one, when you and I met and I broke my ankle. I've never told them about the others; they would freak out. It's bad enough my being a police officer in the day job without them imagining I investigate murders in my spare time. Even if I did tell them, they would think I was making it up. I can hardly believe it myself sometimes."

"Quite," said Marjorie, eyes twinkling with humour. "Investigating murder is an unusual hobby, I grant you."

"They don't know much about Carlos's dangerous investigations, either. We just tell them the funny stories from his more mundane work."

"I see. In that case, we might need to step back from this one, even if it does turn out to be suspicious. I agree with your mother: I hope it isn't Mrs Franks's daughter."

"*We* most certainly will stay out of it either way, but whether *I* do is another matter," said Rachel.

Marjorie elected to ignore the comment and continued, "Well, let's just wait and see. We might have misinterpreted what was happening. Perhaps the woman did faint. It must be boiling hot beneath those habits. I was hot in there myself."

Before Rachel had the opportunity to retort that her father was unlikely to give the last rites to someone who had merely fainted, Susan returned and the teas arrived simultaneously. The waiter poured while they waited for him to leave.

"I've just been speaking to a woman in the ladies, and she says someone died in the church service this morning. Your poor father, Rachel. I don't think anyone has ever died during one of his services."

"I hardly think the two events are related," laughed Marjorie.

"Besides, Mum, you're forgetting Mr Brown."

"I'm not sure he counts."

"Oh, do tell. What happened to Mr Brown?" asked Marjorie.

"He was the churchwarden when I was a child. A strange man – Dad inherited him from the previous vicar and tolerated him. We discovered he had a thing for the communion wine, which was always going missing. I was forever asking Dad why Brownie – as we used to call him – had a red nose. He told me it was because he worked outdoors a lot. Anyway, Dad finally gave him the sack after finding him unconscious behind the altar with empty bottles of communion wine scattered around."

"And did he die during a service?"

"Not quite," answered Susan, taking over the story. "He stumbled into church during one of Brendan's sermons – a good one too, even though I say so myself – rather worse for wear and was asked to leave by his replacement, a burly man who didn't take any nonsense. Sadly, he was found dead after the service in the grounds of the church. Brendan felt terrible about the whole matter."

"I'm sure it wouldn't have been his fault."

"It wasn't," Rachel took over again. "Brownie died of liver failure following years of alcohol abuse. His family said he had refused help at every turn, and they were relieved it was over. They even thanked my father for firing him, as it had at least given him the opportunity to seek help. After the shock of losing his job, he sobered up for a short time, but it wasn't long before he returned to his old ways."

"Here's your father now," said Susan.

Brendan Prince walked slowly. His face was ashen. The usual calm demeanour was missing when he joined them. Running his left hand through his shock of curly brown hair, he almost fell on to the cushioned bench next to Susan, exhaling deeply as he did so. Rachel was worried, but didn't say anything.

Marjorie took control and ordered more tea and a brandy. Rachel's father held his hand up to protest, but Marjorie was firm.

"You've had a shock. It will help settle the nerves."

Brendan nodded in appreciation. "Perhaps a small one then."

Once the brandy and tea arrived, Brendan drank the alcohol, then looked up at Rachel.

"I've seen some things, Rachel, but I don't know how you and Sarah cope."

"What happened, Dad?" she pressed gently.

"After the service ended, I came down from the stage and was standing at the front with Sarah and Gareth, the pleasant second officer who congratulated me on a fine service. All of a sudden we heard a loud scream coming from somewhere in the third row. The young nuns were sitting there, so it came as a double shock to hear the primal shriek coming from that direction – they hadn't said a word all through the service. They didn't join in the prayers or sing any of the hymns, which I found unusual and a little disconcerting.

"Anyway, we hurried towards a cluster of them surrounding a distressed young woman who was shaking the nun seated next to her. Pandemonium broke out as the others in the party realised that the young woman had been taken seriously ill. At first we thought it was a faint. After officers and stewards moved people away so that we could attend to her, Sarah explained it was more serious. She could barely feel a pulse.

"Someone radioed for emergency assistance, and Sarah asked the officers to move the young nun out of the confined space into the nearest aisle. It was a bit of a struggle because they had to hustle the other nuns along the row. Once she was on the floor, we realised how serious the situation was."

Brendan took a sip of tea with trembling hands.

"A horrible film covered her eyes, like something you see in one of those awful movies where nerve agents or some apocalyptic virus is released into the atmosphere. She was also – close your ears, dear…" he turned to his wife, "…foaming at the mouth. Sarah ordered everyone to stand back at this point. Except the young nun wouldn't let go of my hand. She pulled me to her and held her crucifix, pleading with me through mumbles for the last rites, so I did as she wished. Afterwards she whispered something that sounded rather strange."

Rachel found herself holding her breath. "What?"

Her father looked around to ensure no-one else was listening.

"She whispered, 'Armageddon'."

Rachel remained silent, puzzled as to what that might mean.

"Do you know if they got her round?" asked Marjorie.

"I'm afraid not. She stopped breathing moments later, before the medical team arrived. Sarah began resuscitation, and once the chief medical officer arrived with some other medics, one of them ushered me away. I sat at the front of the theatre trying to compose myself and left them to it.

"Your man, Waverley, arrived with the doctor. He sat with me for a while after speaking to a few of the nuns that had witnessed their sister's collapse and asked me for a brief statement. He says he will come by our room later, Susan." He looked towards his wife.

"Well, clearly they don't think it's any contagious disease or they wouldn't have allowed you out," Marjorie stated with a hint of relief in her voice.

"I heard Sarah suggest she was having a fit, but I don't know any more than that."

"Of course that would explain it. If she had epilepsy and suffered a bad fit, it would cause those symptoms. Some people even stop taking their medicines. I'm so sorry, Dad. Not a good start to your cruising experience. I don't suppose you found out her name or anything about the order?"

"Her name was Easter, I think. I heard the girl shaking her, trying to wake her up, call her by that name. I don't know anything about the order, other than the strange behaviour throughout the service, but then I'm not a cloistered sort of vicar."

Rachel and Marjorie exchanged glances, pleased that her name wasn't Jacintha.

"What a beautiful name," remarked Susan.

"The girl was beautiful to match the name. She can't have been any older than Rachel and Sarah – in fact, I'd say she was a few years younger." A tear threatened to fall down Brendan's face. "All the young women were lovely. I heard Gareth joking about it being such a waste."

"We did remark on their looks ourselves. But, tragic as the whole thing has been, these things happen. I think we should try to put it behind us," said Marjorie, attracting Rachel's eye, urging her to concur. Susan was visibly paling.

"Marjorie's right. Dad, Mum, let's try to forget about it."

Rachel had every intention of finding out more about the mysterious death of this nun and her strange final declaration. For now it was important to help her parents move on from what they had just witnessed. Her mother appeared pleased that the dead girl's mother wasn't Gloria, but she was still someone's daughter.

"I agree." Brendan sat up straighter. "Your mother and I are going to a talk on the history of the Virgin Islands. Shall we meet up for lunch afterwards?"

"We also need to find out what that girl's surname was, Brendan. We met a woman after the service who was convinced she was her daughter, although the first name doesn't fit. I promised I'd find out for her."

Rachel's father nodded. "Of course, but I'm pleased to say it's unlikely to be her. Rachel can ask Sarah later."

"That's settled then. Marjorie and I will go up to the Sky View Lounge and read. Meet you at 1.30? We have an art class this afternoon."

"Okay, we'll see you then."

Rachel was happy to see her father perk up. Now he had a copy of the *Coral News* in his hand, studying it methodically, she was no longer worried about him.

"We need to meet up with Sarah as soon as possible so that we can put Mum and Gloria's minds at rest," Rachel said to Marjorie as they made their way upstairs via the lifts. They used the central viewing lift, from where Rachel saw a concerned looking chief of security marching through the public areas of the main atrium.

"Waverley looks flustered." Rachel nodded her head down in his direction.

"Oh dear, that is not good news," Marjorie remarked. "He's got *that* look about him."

"I do hope it's not murder, I was really looking forward to a Caribbean cruise without any mishaps or crime. It's bad enough Carlos not being here. I don't think we can become embroiled in an investigation with my parents on board. Mum wouldn't like it."

"I quite agree, Rachel. As I've already said, in this instance, it would be better to curb our involvement, regardless of how the poor woman died. I'm sure His Lordship can handle a case without us for once."

Rachel laughed at Marjorie's pet name for Jack Waverley. The relationship between her elderly friend and the chief of security was at times volatile and he was unlikely to welcome their involvement. It would make sense to step back this time and enjoy the break.

"Perhaps she died from natural causes. I was once called to an incident where a young woman almost died from an epileptic fit following a brawl in a pub. Maybe she did have severe epilepsy, or even a brain tumour. I remember Sarah telling me about a student in her nurse training who died out of the blue after a tumour burst."

"There you are, then. But on that pleasant note—" Marjorie squeezed Rachel's arm as they stepped out of the lift, "—even if it is suspicious, we should leave well alone. It worries me thinking there might be a nun killer on board – all murder is nasty, but there is something quite heinous about those who would kill a nun."

"I agree. It takes a particular kind of evil to murder men or women of the church."

Rachel felt her pulse racing, an unusual fear of malice weighing over her heart.

Chapter 4

The seminar room beside the art gallery was almost empty when Rachel and Marjorie arrived for their first art lesson. Marjorie had been keen to use the sea days productively and Rachel had always wanted to try her hand at painting, so they had booked the class after boarding the day before. Rachel had seen some of Marjorie's sketches and watercolours and knew her friend was already a fine artist.

The tables had been arranged to accommodate eight people at each. A group of four was already seated at one of the six tables and Rachel was about to join them when Marjorie nudged her.

"I think this one will provide better light for my ageing eyes," she laughed and Rachel followed her to a table where they sat by themselves. Marjorie indicated with her head the reason for her choice. A gathering of blue habits waited outside.

"What were you saying before lunch?" Rachel said, smirking.

"I don't know what you mean. The light here is better, that's all."

Rachel was pleased with Marjorie's choice as it happened. While it was indeed lighter, it also gave them a clear view of the waiting nuns.

"I wonder if they are joining the class," she said enthusiastically.

"Now who's not sticking to our pledge? They have found their voices, from what I can hear."

Marjorie was right. The group congregating outside the room was one of excitable young women on holiday. Any sadness at the loss of the sister appeared to be lacking.

Another four people entered and joined the first four. They were followed in by a group of eight elderly people who looked as though they all knew each other. Afterwards, the nuns entered, speaking in excited tones, some occasionally switching to Spanish. Rachel assumed from their complexion and accent that they originated from South America.

Five of the nuns joined Rachel and Marjorie's table. Marjorie introduced herself and Rachel to the two women opposite, and one of them politely reciprocated.

"I'm Cheryl, sometimes known as Cherry, but not so much these days." She glanced anxiously at an older nun at the far end of the table. Cheryl looked around the same age as Rachel, a couple of inches shorter with large cat-green eyes, cute freckles over her nose and cheeks, and a diamond-shaped face. She appeared nervous. Rachel smiled, encouraging her to continue, but she said no more.

"And you?" Marjorie asked the girl next to Cheryl.

"Letitia."

Rachel had already summed up that Letitia was a couple of years older than Cheryl. Her pale face was round and she had beautiful aquamarine eyes; her accent was Eastern European. Looking around, Rachel noticed what her mother had pointed out this morning: that each woman was beautiful. Perfect, in fact; not even a blemish on any of the faces she could see.

No further introductions were possible at this stage as the course leader introduced himself. If he hadn't told them he was the course leader, Rachel would have guessed anyway because of the way

48

he looked. His demeanour was vivacious and his clothes shouted arty: bright red trousers and a multicoloured t-shirt loose at the neck, revealing some long grey chest hair that made her cringe. He introduced himself as Dwaine. She summed him up as being late fifties with dyed blond hair reaching below his shoulders and a fringe that hung over his right eye, causing him to throw his head back every so often. Occasionally he brushed it back with his hand, followed by a tilt of the head just like she had seen the celebrity gardener Charlie Dimmock do on numerous television programmes.

Rachel liked Dwaine immediately. His extrovert personality filled the room and he was clearly good at what he did as his paintings were mounted on easels behind where he stood.

"Oh I do wish he'd stop messing with his hair," Marjorie said. "He needs to see a barber pronto."

Rachel laughed; she could tell Marjorie liked him despite the hair issue. She laughed at his jokes and listened to his instruction, paying particular attention to any technical detail. He was winning over the whole room, even the nuns from what she could see.

"Art is about what you see. You don't have to paint what you see in front of you, although when there is a room full of beauty, it's hard not to." An embarrassed chuckle from some of the nuns was met with a scowl by others. "It can be what you see in your head, and that's often where true creativity originates. For some, it is the Picasso type of lines and colours; for others it can be splashes of colour that may not make sense to anyone but the artist. Some of the greatest works were ridiculed by those who didn't see the genius the artist had created."

Dwaine waxed lyrical for a while before sighing.

"And for others, art is about painting fruit." The whole room broke into joyful laughter at his clear disdain for still life painting. "But I'm going to teach you some principles that you need to begin with before you start experimenting."

"There's a man who doesn't lack in confidence," said Marjorie as they started some practical work.

Despite the joke about fruit, Dwaine had placed a bowl of artificial fruit on three of the tables and flowers on the others. Each artist had to try to reproduce the still life on paper. The room was now alive with people chatting and laughing. Cheryl talked easily to Marjorie, but every so often she cast an anxious glance towards the older nun. Letitia, the girl opposite Rachel, concentrated on her drawing.

Rachel spoke to the young woman sitting to her right. "That's really good," she said. "I've always been hopeless at art. History was my thing."

"I've always liked art. It's a gift from God. We believe art allows the spirit to become closer to the heavenly. Sister Murdoch actively encourages us to express ourselves through all forms of art: painting, sewing, classical music and reading."

Rachel had never considered sewing to be art, but she supposed that dress designers were artists in their own way. Carlos's sister was certainly artistic when it came to interior design.

"Who's Sister Murdoch?"

"The lady on my right at the end of the table." Rachel had already assumed that the serious older woman was one of the leaders of the order. She couldn't get a good look at her, as she was on the same side as her and Marjorie, but she noticed the difference in habit and age.

"That sounds interesting. I do appreciate art, I'm just not very creative myself. I'm Rachel, by the way, and this is Marjorie." Rachel leaned back to introduce her friend.

"I'm Sister Lee."

Rachel found this young woman a little too religious for her. Sometimes religion imprisoned people rather than setting them free, she felt, and in this woman's case, that's what she detected, but she decided it was none of her business. She made a quick assessment of Sister Lee, who hadn't volunteered a first name, while Marjorie attempted to engage her in friendly conversation.

The nun was also late twenties and pretty, but the serious face and sharp lines tarnished her beauty. Her skin was tanned and she had light brown eyes. Judging by the accent, Rachel assumed she originated from Ireland.

"Her name's Blethyn," said a girl on the opposite side of the table to Sister Lee. "She can be a bit full of herself sometimes, can't you, Blethyn?" Emphasis on the first name.

Blethyn focussed on her sketch and blanked the girl, who spoke with a South American accent.

"I'm Angeline Elwood."

In spite of Angeline's comments about Blethyn, she was just as serious. She was younger than Rachel, mid-twenties with dark brown, almost black eyes and olive skin. Rachel detected a prickly note in her voice and suspected she was digging at Blethyn rather than speaking to her. There was clearly some rivalry within this holy order and the nuns were not above sniping at each other.

"Ignore those two," said Cheryl. "They are close really, but they like to pretend they're not."

"You should be more careful what you say," said Blethyn. "You know what the Bible says about a loose tongue."

Rachel was picking up on more than a bit of friendly banter; there was angst among these few women, which made her wonder whether it ran through the whole order, and more importantly, whether it was enough to lead to murder.

"And what about what it says about love?" whispered Marjorie to Rachel while Cheryl and Blethyn continued their sparring match. Cheryl was no match for the serious Blethyn and appeared to be regretting getting into the conversation in the first place. Her hands shook as she held the charcoal pencil in one hand and the paper with the other. Rachel noticed Letitia nudge Cheryl, who coloured red as she turned her attention to the end of the table where Rachel could only assume that Sister Murdoch was glaring at the young nun. The corners of Angeline's mouth turned upwards and a knowing glance passed between her and Blethyn, who smirked openly.

I would call that entrapment, Rachel thought. They had baited Cheryl to react, but was it just because they didn't like her – a bit of one-upmanship – or was it to make themselves look better? She suspected it was a bit of both, but whether it was just high-school type bullying or something deeper, she would need to find out.

No-one had mentioned the death of the poor young woman this morning, but that could just be because they wanted to forget about it.

"That is very good, excellent work."

Rachel realised Dwaine was standing behind her and Marjorie and she knew he wasn't referring to her wonky apples, so he must be referring to Marjorie's exact copy of the fruit bowl, with a few additions.

"Wow, Marjorie! That's lovely," she said.

Dwaine turned his attention to Rachel's work. "Hmm, keep trying."

Their teacher worked his way around the table, complimenting each of the nuns in turn for their various offerings. Blethyn stiffened when he enthusiastically praised Cheryl's work and held it up as an example to another table. Cheryl was oblivious to the daggers she was drawing from Angeline and Blethyn. Cheryl had told the others how good their own work was, even complimenting Blethyn, which Rachel thought was generous.

The class ended and Rachel and
Marjorie headed towards Creams
Patisserie for afternoon tea. This was a
favourite haunt of Rachel's and she'd
often met up with Sarah there to discuss
cases in the past.

"What did you think of that exhibition,
and I don't mean the drawing?" asked
Marjorie.

"There's no doubt some of them don't
like each other, but it happens. They are,
after all, just a group of young women.
There are bound to be factions."

"Yes, but you would think they would
try to paper over the cracks in public,
wouldn't you? If they are like that with
strangers, I would imagine it's much
worse in private."

"I can see what you're thinking,
Marjorie Snellthorpe. There would need
to be a huge leap from rivalry – even
malicious rivalry – to murder."

"You don't fool me, Rachel. You're just as intrigued as I am. Admit it, there's more to this order than they let on."

"Okay, I will admit it made me wonder, but until we find out whether the woman called Easter died of natural causes or not, it's just a group of women behaving like children."

"Yes, you're quite right, but I wouldn't want to spend too much time with that Blethyn – too heavenly minded to be of any earthly use, if you ask me. The halo slipped, though, when Dwaine praised Cheryl, didn't it?"

"You noticed that too? Yes, Blethyn went rigid – I braved a quick glance and there was rage in that face. I wouldn't want to get on the wrong side of her. Perhaps she joined the order to deal with anger issues or something. She was in awe of Sister Murdoch, though."

"Was that the older woman at the end? Crooked nose and pale skin, not to mention the cat's eyes? In my opinion, she's more dangerous than the lot of them."

"How can you describe her so clearly? I couldn't even see her from where I was sitting."

"I went to get a glass of water from the bar – you were concentrating on your drawing after Dwaine had been rather unkind about it, I think."

"No, he was right. I was rubbish, but I'm willing to try. I did like him, though."

"Me too, but you're changing the subject."

"Which is?"

"Murder, my dear. That young woman was murdered."

Rachel's heart sank because she couldn't agree more with her friend.

Chapter 5

Rachel was dressing for dinner when there was a knock at the door. She opened it to find Sarah hopping up and down. They shrieked in unison and hugged each other in the corridor before Sarah followed Rachel into the room, talking excitedly.

"I couldn't wait to see you, but am I disturbing you?"

"No, I was just getting ready for dinner. We're meeting up in the wine bar for pre-dinner drinks. Are you going to join us?"

"I have evening surgery to do soon, but after that I hand over the on-call bag to Brigitte. I can meet you in the Jazz Bar later, if that suits?"

"That would be great. My parents and Marjorie are itching to catch up with you."

"Likewise. How was the flight and the overnight stay in New York?"

"It wasn't bad at all, not too much turbulence coming over. We spent the afternoon shopping, then crashed before joining the ship yesterday."

"I bet your parents enjoyed that."

"They did, but it's all about the cruise for them. I realise you met with Dad this morning after the service when that nun collapsed and died. Dad says the poor woman had a fit."

Sarah slumped into a chair and looked disbelievingly at Rachel.

"Please don't tell me it's suspicious." Rachel and Marjorie's assessment could be right after all.

"I'm afraid it might be. The body has been returned to New York for a postmortem and toxicology."

"In that case, you'll be pleased to hear that Marjorie and I have agreed – even if it is suspicious – we won't get involved. So, unlikely as it may seem, on this occasion I'm not going to ask too many questions."

Sarah's eyebrows hit the ceiling and her eyes opened wide. "Seriously? Well I couldn't be more pleased to hear that news, if you mean it, Rachel. We don't know for sure yet that there is anything untoward, but Graham wasn't happy with the film that formed over the sclera of her eyes, or the manner of her death. A postmortem would have been performed anyway due to the unexpected sudden death."

"Dad mentioned the eyes. How are the other nuns taking it, do you know?"

"To be honest, they seem to have disregarded the whole thing. One of the women in charge, a Sister Murdoch, told Graham that death comes to us all and although they are incredibly saddened by the loss of one of their own – a sadness he couldn't see, by the way – they will continue with their pilgrimage."

Dr Graham Bentley, the chief medical officer on board the *Coral Queen,* was a competent and caring doctor. Rachel couldn't help thinking that if he thought there was something amiss, there probably was.

"Marjorie and I met some of the nuns this afternoon. They had lost the silence of this morning. We encountered this Sister Murdoch – Marjorie didn't take to her at all."

"Did you speak to her then? I have to say that doesn't sound like you staying out of this, Rachel Prince."

"They were in our art class, as a matter of fact, and some of them sat at our table, including Sister Murdoch. And no, we didn't speak to her, but we did speak to a few of the others. There's a lot of underlying tension among the women we spoke to, that I can say."

"Oh dear. That doesn't sound good. I am so hoping it's not murder this time, Rachel."

"Me too. Is that what they are doing on board a cruise ship, then? You mentioned a pilgrimage – where to?"

"St Kitts, apparently. That's what Sister Murdoch told Graham, anyway. I think he said it was something to do with Brimstone Hill."

Rachel gulped as her brain went into overdrive. First the mention of Armageddon, and now Brimstone, both associated with the end of the world, according to the Book of Revelation. She shook her head to dispel any such thoughts and felt pleased not to be getting involved with a case that might turn out to be too weird to contemplate.

"Are you all right, Rachel? You've gone pale."

"Sorry, my mind wandered for a moment, but I'm fine. I thought Brimstone Hill Fortress was related to war and defence, that's all. We booked a trip there because Dad and I are interested in its history."

"I'll take your word for what it's famous for. It's not somewhere I've visited when in the Caribbean. I usually head for the beaches if I get time off. Joining you will be my first time there. Are you sure you're all right?"

Rachel was shaken, but she didn't understand why. "I guess it's the shock of someone dying right in front of Dad. Although he takes funerals, he's only present at expected deaths when called out to parishioners. I do wish Carlos was here. I miss him when stuff like this happens. How's Jason, by the way?"

"My fiancé is as wonderful as ever." Sarah's eyes lit up at the mention of Jason, a security officer on board ship. They had got engaged on Christmas Day towards the end of Rachel's last cruise. "He'll join us tonight, if that's okay with you?"

"Of course, Marjorie will be delighted. She liked him when they met on land, and Mum and Dad would like to meet him so they can take home news to your parents."

"That's settled then. See you at nine-thirty."

Rachel hurriedly finished dressing for dinner, wearing a burgundy cocktail dress and applying a touch of makeup before rushing a few doors down to call on

Marjorie, who was staying in a suite at the stern of the ship. Her parents' room was sandwiched in between.

Marjorie's bright blue eyes shone as she answered the door. Rachel stood back and admired how immaculately dressed her elderly friend was in a purple silk v-necked dress with matching shoes, carrying a white handbag. But the thing Rachel liked most about Marjorie was her snow-white hair. It always looked like she had just stepped out of a classy salon.

"You look wonderful." Rachel leaned down to kiss her friend on the cheek.

"And so do you, Rachel. Your hair has gone even blonder, yet we've hardly been in the sunlight today. I love the waves – is that a new look?"

"Tonged into submission. I like to experiment occasionally."

"Well you look as beautiful as ever, my dear. Have you heard from Sarah? Any news on you know what?"

Seeing the glint in her friend's eye, she detected that Marjorie was already having second thoughts about keeping her nose out of the sudden death they'd witnessed earlier that day. Rachel put her arm through hers.

"She's meeting us in the Jazz Bar at nine-thirty with Jason. She was positively glowing."

"I see. In that case, I look forward to it. Shall we collect your lovely parents?"

"No need." Rachel's mother appeared behind them as they left Marjorie's suite. "We're here."

There was no mention of the events of the morning as they enjoyed a three-course dinner in the main Coral Restaurant. A beautiful sunset was visible through an oval window nearby, but Rachel noticed it was catching her mother's eye, causing her to squint. A couple in their mid-to-late forties was dining at the table for two by the window. The spindly man appeared to notice other people's discomfort, smiling maliciously at a woman in her sixties before pulling the curtain back even further. This caused the glare to become visibly uncomfortable for Rachel's mother, as well as the intended victim.

The sun was clearly bothering the poor woman, who asked the man if he would mind pulling the curtain across a fraction. Rachel studied him in more detail: a tall man with a thin face and short grey hair, dressed in a white suit and black bow tie. The hair was neatly groomed and he wore wire-rimmed spectacles; his sharp, elongated face appeared gaunt.

He turned his head to glare at the woman who had dared ask him to move the curtain. "I'm sure you can bear it for another three minutes," he growled. Following a further polite request, he turned his head to admire the sunset, blanking the woman totally.

"Dressed like a gentleman, but behaving like a hooligan," said Marjorie to Rachel's mother, who had moved her chair away so that the sun couldn't bother her so much. The woman who'd made the request glared in astonishment at the rude man, whose wife appeared oblivious to his behaviour. Rachel noticed they both wore wedding rings.

"There are some very selfish people in the world," Rachel concurred. People at surrounding tables had noticed the brief fracas and murmured disapprovingly at his unusual behaviour. It was at least ten minutes before the sun no longer caused

Rachel's mother and the other lady discomfort, and all the while Rachel sat fuming, resisting the temptation to march over to the window and pull the curtain over herself. Such a small incident was ruining her evening.

Marjorie squeezed her arm.

"People like that aren't worth the effort, dear. I'll have a word with the maître d on the way out to ensure it doesn't happen again."

Rachel nodded, quelling her rising anger. "A swift karate chop wouldn't go amiss, though." She smiled at Marjorie. Rachel was a karate black belt, but would not exercise the skill other than in self-defence. Marjorie laughed.

At that moment, a small group of the blue nun contingent exited the restaurant, and Rachel's anger turned to intrigue as she noticed the spindly man slip a piece of paper into one of the nuns' hands as they passed. Rachel jolted upright, uncertain of what she had just witnessed.

"Are you all right, Rachel?" asked her father, who was seated opposite her.

"Yes, sorry, I thought I saw someone I knew."

"One of the nuns?" asked her mother, eyeing her suspiciously. "Rachel, I do hope you're not going to allow your inquisitiveness to get the better of you. I would like to forget the events of this morning, and so would your father."

"I don't know what you mean. One of them reminded me of someone I met at university, but it's not her."

"Well at least the sun's gone down," her mother answered, changing the subject as she moved her chair back into a more comfortable position. But Rachel could sense that Marjorie was not fooled for an instant.

Chapter 6

"What was that about over dinner?"
Marjorie quizzed. She and Rachel had
headed to the Jazz Bar after dinner to
meet up with Sarah and Jason, while
Brendan and Susan, exhausted by the
eventful day, had elected to get an early
night.

"I'm not sure. I thought I noticed
something odd, but it was probably
nothing."

Before Rachel could explain what she
thought she might have witnessed, she
heard a cheerful Filipino accent coming
from behind them.

"Rachel, Lady Snellthorpe, it's such a
pleasure to see you again." The familiar

small frame of Bernard, one of the other nurses who worked with Sarah and had become a good friend of Rachel's, drew her into a hug. "Even if I hadn't known you were on board, I would have guessed it as soon as a body turned up in the morgue." Bernard's flippant but dark humour could break through any tension, and had done so on many previous occasions. "And you, Lady Snellthorpe, are becoming just as much a danger magnet to have on board our otherwise banal cruise liner."

"Away with you, and less of the Lady, please. Call me Marjorie."

"Okay, Marjorie. Sarah's over there with her man." Bernard nodded towards a booth on the far side of the bar. "I'm waiting for Brigitte, and then we'll join you. I can't wait to catch up and see what you've uncovered so far."

Marjorie pulled Rachel away before she could protest and walked her towards Sarah. Jason stood as the women arrived. Both he and Sarah were in uniform. Jason and Sarah had been dating for almost a year before their engagement; Rachel liked him and was pleased to see the relationship appeared to be flourishing, despite a few bumps along the way.

Sarah kissed Marjorie and they sat down in the relative privacy of the booth. Lively jazz melodies filled the air, along with the buzz from conversations of people enjoying their holiday.

"I've explained to Jason that you promised to have no involvement whatsoever with investigating the death from this morning." Sarah lowered her voice so that others nearby wouldn't hear.

"That's good to hear, the boss will be grateful. It's lovely to see you ladies again," said Jason. Ordinarily Rachel

would have wanted to take advantage of
Jason's position as part of the ship's
security team to question him further, but
she decided for her parents' sakes that she
wouldn't. Her only dilemma was whether
to mention the curious note exchange that
she might have witnessed in the dining
room, but by now she'd almost convinced
herself it had been her imagination.

Easy conversation flowed, even more
so after Bernard and Brigitte, a French
nurse who also worked in the medical
team, joined them. Rachel felt at home
with the medical team and many of the
security team, having encountered both
regularly during her previous cruises.
Brigitte kept Bernard under control, and
each time he tried to bring up the nun's
death, she changed the subject, not
wanting to discuss such things. Brigitte
was not a fan of Bernard's gutter humour,
as she called it.

But Bernard persisted. "You know the death is unlikely to be natural though, not with Rachel Prince and Marjorie Snellthorpe on board."

"Stop it, Bernard. You should grow up," snapped Brigitte. "Death is not funny."

One couldn't help smiling along with Bernard's sunny personality. The mischievous male nurse countered the rather serious Brigitte and made for an interesting working relationship, although this time, Sarah was also frowning at Bernard.

Brigitte's radio went off towards the end of the evening, calling her away to assist Alex Romano, the junior doctor on board, with a patient who had fallen over.

"Drunk, I expect." She shrugged her shoulders as she said goodnight. Soon afterwards, the others decided it was time to leave.

"I'm on the night shift," said Jason, kissing Sarah on the cheek. "I'd better go and relieve Ravanos."

"I'm going to bed; it's been a long day," said Sarah. "Goodnight, guys."

"I'm heading to the crew bar to make sure there are no fights," said Bernard, rolling his eyes.

Rachel laughed. "Well don't give them any of your stingers, then."

"My secret cocktail," he answered Marjorie's enquiring look.

"They'll probably be sticking to Blue Nun," replied Marjorie with a chuckle, her humour as wicked as Bernard's at times. Bernard returned a baffled look before heading on his way, but Rachel couldn't help but laugh, recognising the name of a popular German wine.

Rachel sat back satisfied after Bernard had left. "It's like a second home."

"I know what you mean," agreed Marjorie. "I feel I know these people as well as I know any of my rapidly diminishing circle back home."

Marjorie had lost a few friends over the winter months.

"I was sorry to hear about Mrs Fleming passing away."

"Me too. She was one of my oldest friends. Of course, death is to be expected at my age; it's just that there are fewer and fewer who remember me as a young woman. I haven't always been elderly and infirm, you know."

"You are far from infirm, Marjorie Snellthorpe, but I think I understand what you're saying."

"Still, I have you and Carlos to keep me young, so I can't complain. Now, you were going to tell me what happened in the restaurant this evening following that ignorant man's behaviour. Did it have something to do with the blue nuns?" She chuckled again.

"Marjorie Snellthorpe, you can be as bad as Bernard sometimes."

"Nonsense! A good wine it is, too. White, I believe. But you're trying to change the subject. What happened?"

Rachel laughed. "I'm not certain anything happened; it was over in an instant, but I thought I saw that obnoxious man pass a note to one of the nuns."

"If you thought you saw it, that's good enough for me. It gives us something to go on, doesn't it? Bernard did manage to hint in between young Brigitte gagging him that the death is suspicious, which confirms our belief."

"Yes, Sarah said the same thing earlier. Apparently Dr Bentley is worried, and the nun's body is on its way back to New York for post mortem." Then Rachel, seeing the look of eager interest on

Marjorie's face, pulled herself together. "But Sarah also said that would happen for any sudden death, it doesn't necessarily mean it was murder. And what part of our not getting involved does this conversation meet?" Rachel chuckled. "Come on, I think it's time for bed."

But as the two friends walked back to their staterooms in companionable silence, Rachel couldn't help thinking she was already being drawn into yet another murder investigation, no matter how much she tried to convince herself otherwise.

Chapter 7

Jack Waverley, the chief security officer, was struggling to get to sleep after the events of the morning. It wasn't every day he was faced with the death of a beautiful young woman with her whole life ahead of her, and a nun at that. It had unsettled him.

Almost as soon as he did drift off, he was awoken by a telephone call. He checked the bedside clock: 4am. Could this be the call that would confirm Graham Bentley's fears that the death of the nun, Sister Easter Balch, was not natural?

"Yes?"

"We have a coroner from New York on the line."

"Okay, put him through."

"Sorry to disturb you so late, but I was told you wanted results day or night."

"No problem. Do you have a cause of death?"

The coroner's voice on the other end of the phone sounded weary. "We're not certain yet. Some form of digitalis, I suspect, but it could also be a neurotoxin; I don't like to guess. We'll have to await further toxicology results."

"Were there any signs pointing to murder?"

"There were no bruises to the body if that's what you mean, other than a cracked rib on X-ray. That would have been caused by the attempted resuscitation, I read the report from your ship's doctor. It's hard to say otherwise, but if it's a digitalis overdose, it would be unlikely to be from tablets of her own. I can find no evidence of a heart condition from the medical history. The only other thing was early signs of liver damage, unusual for a woman her age, which indicates recent and prolonged heavy drinking."

"How recent?"

"Within the past few years, but there was no alcohol in the stomach, so the death was unrelated. There's no mention of a drink problem in the records I've checked."

"Can you at least say whether you think it's murder, and if so, how the substance was administered?"

"The substance was ingested. I can find no evidence of injection or forced ingestion, so it's difficult to say. If it is a digitalis overdose, you would need to know whether she had access to the pills, whether she took them intentionally or by accident, and whether they were slipped into her food or something."

"Thank you, Doctor. I wouldn't have thought of that." This man was becoming irritating. "How long before death would the drug have been taken?"

The coroner sighed. "I can't tell you that for certain. As I've explained, it would depend on what was administered and whether it was digitalis or something else. Digitalis acts quite quickly, within minutes if the dose is high enough, but slower if a lower dose is taken. We need to be certain. I'm sending away a sample of the stomach contents."

"Best guess?" Waverley persisted.

"Within the hour if high-dose digitalis, several hours if lower, but as I've explained, it could have been longer or shorter. She seemingly went into cardiac arrest."

"Why didn't she move or try to call out for help before it got too late?"

"That, Chief, is for you to find out. I just look at cause of death. The whys and wherefores are down to you. Perhaps she couldn't."

"Thanks for the reminder." Waverley sighed heavily.

"There is one thing you should know, though."

This should be interesting coming from this anorak. Waverley scrunched his face, expecting a wry joke, but asked anyway.

"What's that, Doctor?"

"The NYPD is taking an overly keen interest in the case considering it happened at sea. I've had at least three phone calls and a visit. If I didn't know better—"

"You'd think she was one of theirs." Waverley finished the sentence.

"Precisely, but no-one's admitting it. There's no two-way information sharing as such, I'm just guessing from the level of interest coming my way. You should expect to hear from a Detective Duncan Rodrigues, he's the one who called round personally. A man not to be crossed, so watch out. I've had dealings with him in the past. He's not averse to skirting round the law to catch a criminal."

"Thanks for the heads-up. Let me know as soon as you get the toxicology back, will you?"

"Of course. Now if there's nothing else, I've got two fatal gunshot recipients to attend to. Goodnight, Chief Waverley."

Not waiting for a reply, the sleepy coroner put the telephone down.

Waverley sat on the edge of the bed, mulling over the conversation, particularly the NYPD interest. What, if anything, had the NYPD to do with this woman's death? Perhaps the girl was someone's relative. Something told him there was more to the death than a straightforward murder – not that murder was ever that simple.

Why would a young nun be murdered on board a cruise ship in broad daylight? And why in church, of all places?

Waverley was not superstitious himself, but many sailors were. This death would not go down well among the crew, and even less so if there was any suspicion of the dark arts or some cultish reason behind it. He almost hoped she had been an undercover cop as he rubbed his hand through his thinning hair. He didn't like this situation at all.

Why can't people get killed somewhere else? And why does it always happen on the Coral Queen when a certain Rachel Prince is on board? She's a murder magnet, there's no denying it.

"Are you all right?" Brenda stirred, then sat up and put her arms around him.

"Sorry," Waverley turned to his wife, "I've just had bad news about the girl that died. The death's not straightforward; it's suspicious at best, murder at worst. Seems she didn't have epilepsy and may have taken or been given something that caused a heart attack."

"Oh, Jack, I'm sorry. I suppose that means you're not going to get much rest until you've found out what's going on. You did warn me that your young friend Rachel Prince always attracted trouble."

"She certainly does that, although I can't hold her responsible for any of the past events – or this one, for that matter. It just seems she is always around when there's a murder committed."

"If it is foul play. Why do you think anyone would kill a young nun? From what I hear, this particular group of nuns would be better suited to life as models!"

It hadn't gone unnoticed among the crew how good-looking the young women in the holy order were. Waverley couldn't help wondering why they were all so pretty himself, but he was in no mood for jokes. Ignoring Brenda's attempt at humour, he replied thoughtfully.

"There are a few reasons that someone might kill this particular nun – her name was Easter Balch. The first is just basic racism – she was black, but I can't believe that's the case as we are truly international on board a cruise ship."

"Like the United Nations," agreed Brenda.

"So could it be religiophobia? Someone who has it in for the nuns because they're religious?"

"In which case she would have been picked at random rather than specifically, you mean?"

"Yes, someone who has it in for nuns – it happens. If she was the intended victim, it could be a personal grudge against her or the order she is with." He neglected to say that she could have been an undercover cop. Brenda was discreet, but there would be a lot of talk and he wanted to save anything slipping out that might be best kept under wraps.

"I have heard some people can be afraid of nuns."

"Sphenisciphobia." Waverley spent hours doing crosswords when he wasn't solving crimes aboard the *Coral*. "But people with a phobia would be more likely to avoid them than kill them."

"That's true. You don't think the reason is obvious, do you. Are you planning on bringing Rachel Prince in on your investigation?"

"You can read me well, Brenda, that's why I love you so much. I don't know why things always happen when Rachel Prince is on board, right enough. Under normal circumstances I'd be warning her off, but I've got a feeling I might need her for this case."

"Why is that?"

"Well, if there's something sinister going on, either within or without the order, I can hardly infiltrate a bunch of nuns, can I?" He laughed. "She fits the profile of this rather unusual religious order. As you say, they are all young and pretty, similar height and weight. It's almost as if they have been selected accordingly, and Rachel is young, beautiful and about the right height."

"Now you're making me jealous."

He turned back and kissed her. "You're the most beautiful woman in the world to me, but she would blend in perfectly if they need a new recruit. I'm thinking they have been meticulous in planning their pilgrimage and may have chosen a very specific number to fulfil whatever it is they're up to. If so, they will need a replacement for Miss Balch. Even if they don't, Rachel's father is a vicar and witnessed the death. He and Rachel have a better chance of getting close to these women than I do. I don't understand religious types. This sort of thing gives me the creeps."

"That sounds rather sinister, Jack. Are you sure it's not just a simple case of jealousy or envy? I'm sure nuns aren't immune to either."

"In a way, I hope that's the case, but I need to be prepared if it's not. I want the replacement to come from within if I'm right."

"Wouldn't they be suspicious?"

"First of all I need to find out if I'm right. It might be nothing to do with their order at all. I have a feeling that in a few hours I will know more. Now, darling, you go back to sleep; you've got a long day ahead. I'm going to get up and give Dr Graham Bentley an early morning call."

"He's going to love you," she said quietly. Then she pulled the duvet back over her head and fell asleep almost immediately.

Waverley kissed the back of her head before taking a shower, pulling on his uniform and making his way a few doors down the staff corridor to the chief medical officer's room. The door opened almost immediately he'd knocked.

"Sorry to wake you, Graham. It's about Easter Balch."

"To be honest, I was awake, going through her records, such as we have. I'm trying to work out why a young woman like that would die suddenly. I can't find any history of epilepsy, so she either had a fit out of nowhere, causing a heart attack, or there's something untoward behind her death."

"I can tell you it wasn't a fit that killed her, but can't tell you for certain the real cause of death at the moment. The coroner believes it was a drug-induced heart attack."

"Oh. Digitalis?"

"How did you know?"

"Digitalis overdose can cause disorientation, fits and cardiac arrest."

Waverley shared the details of the call from the coroner. "I don't know whether he was tired, but I had to drag every sentence out of him."

"You know us medics, Jack. We like to hedge."

"Mm, possibly. Anyway, there you have it. Probable murder or accidental overdose, but actual cause of death remains uncertain."

"I don't like the idea of having a nun killer on board. It could have been suicide, of course."

"If my suspicions are right, she may not have been a nun. That's why I'm here. What more can you tell me about her background?"

"All I've got is a sparse medical record of no significance. As I'm sure you know already, she was twenty-nine, born in Sierra Leone, but had dual United States citizenship. If she wasn't a nun that would explain the body piercing."

"What do you mean?"

"The victim had a bellybutton piercing."

"But don't some women convert later in life?" Waverley coughed, embarrassed. "Do they need to be celibate to join a nunnery?"

"Indeed they can join at any age, but most nuns would not continue to wear such adornment around their navel. It would usually be renounced alongside other worldly paraphernalia. In terms of celibacy, yes, they take a vow of chastity, but not all nuns are virgins these days."

Waverley coughed again. "I see. That does make sense. I think the ones in blue are a bunch of trainees, though. Would that explain the belly jewel?"

"I guess so; they won't have joined in full yet."

"They're called noviciates," said Waverley, enjoying another opportunity to demonstrate his wide vocabulary.

"Yes, comes from the word novice and applies to those training to take holy orders."

Trust Graham Bentley to know the term.

"Right. Have you been able to find a next of kin?"

"No. The contact in her pre-cruise notes is listed as an uncle, but the number doesn't exist. I've requested a full medical file from her American doctor, but that could take some time. Your coroner is more likely to gain access before I do."

"He says she had a damaged liver as well, from heavy drinking."

"That must have been before she became a nun; I believe temperance is a requirement."

"I've applied for a criminal record screen, but if I'm right, I think it will come up blank."

"Okay, the suspense is killing me. Who do you think she was?"

"She was either a young nun who met with a random psychopath on board our ship, a woman with a past that's caught up with her, a member of a religious order that someone has it in for, a sad and lonely woman who killed herself, or – and I believe it more likely – she was an employee of the NYPD."

Waverley was pleased to see he'd caught Graham off guard. It wasn't often he could get one over on the chief medical officer, but this time Graham's jaw dropped.

"Now that is a turn up for the books. I assume we'll know which of those scenarios is in play soon."

"Indeed we will. My main concern is that if she was working for the NYPD, was she working undercover without our knowledge? And if so, will it put other passengers in danger?"

"Questions that no doubt will be answered shortly and something better dealt with on a full stomach. Breakfast?"

"You're on. I'll have a sneaky fry up while Brenda's still asleep."

The two men headed towards the officers' restaurant.

Chapter 8

Rachel was lounging on Marjorie's expansive balcony, soaking up the sun and reading *The Tattooist of Auschwitz* while Marjorie played a game of patience with a pack of playing cards. Their second sea day had begun with a lazy breakfast outside and gone on from there.

"I'm not sure this is good holiday reading, but it's a wonderful love story in spite of the horrific goings-on." Rachel shuddered over the details she had just read.

"Certainly not one to read at bedtime. I prefer a good old Agatha Christie," said Marjorie. "Why don't we order some tea?"

"Great idea," said Rachel, putting the book down, donning a throw and rising to call Mario, the butler who serviced Marjorie's suite. "How do you do that?" she exclaimed as Mario walked in before she'd had the chance to ring. She was convinced Marjorie's room was bugged.

"Do what?" asked Mario, confused.

"Nothing," answered Rachel sheepishly.

"I'm sorry to disturb you, ladies, but Chief Waverley would like to see Rachel in her parents' stateroom."

"Is that so? Well I'm coming too," said Marjorie, putting the playing cards back in their box.

"Do you know what the chief wants, Mario?" asked Rachel, hoping Waverley didn't think she was poking her nose into his investigation.

"No, Miss Rachel, sorry."

"Would you ask them to give me five minutes to dress?"

"And could you take tea for five through to Mr and Mrs Prince's room, Mario, please?" added Marjorie.

"Tea for four, Lady Snellthorpe. Mrs Prince is at the hairdresser's."

Rachel was pleased her mother appeared to be enjoying the break. Both her parents worked hard at home, keeping up with the vicarage and all the church activities as well as participating in committees they were both on. They hadn't had a proper holiday for many years as the church took up all their time and energy.

Rachel came out of Marjorie's bedroom, more suitably attired in crop trousers and a summer vest.

"I didn't want to give Waverley a shock, turning up in a bikini, or he'd have a coughing fit."

Marjorie laughed good-naturedly. "I wonder what he wants."

"He's probably going to pull rank and ask my father to keep me out of his investigation. It suggests the death is suspicious, though, doesn't it? Let's go and find out."

"I do hope your father doesn't agree. I think that man needs help. He has a tendency to blunder around jumping to the wrong conclusions, as you know."

Rachel didn't comment on the fact they had agreed not to meddle; there was no point.

When they arrived in her parents' room, Mario had already delivered tea along with scones and jam. At least the four cups meant Waverley knew to expect Marjorie with her, which would save any awkwardness. The security chief didn't respond well to surprises and his cough would have been a dead giveaway.

Rachel's father looked grim and she recognised the tension in his jaw, which had her worried.

"What is it?" she asked. "Is Mum okay?"

"Yes, she's fine, gone to have her hair permed. I thought the chief had just come to interview me about what I witnessed yesterday morning, but it seems he has something else on his mind. I'll let Chief Waverley explain the reason for this surprise gathering."

"Well, shall we sit down and pour tea first?" said Marjorie. "I do think that news is better delivered over a cup of tea, don't you?"

The men obeyed, sitting on armchairs to one side of the coffee table while Rachel and Marjorie took the sofa. Waverley coughed.

Oh no, thought Rachel as Marjorie nudged her mischievously.

"I'm sorry to intrude on your holiday, Rachel," he coughed again. "I don't know where to start."

"The beginning would be good," prompted Marjorie tersely, not one to encourage procrastination.

Waverley let out a deep sigh. "Yes, the beginning. As you are already aware, a young nun collapsed in the Coral Theatre yesterday morning after the church service and died soon afterwards. Her name was Easter Balch."

"Yes, we heard, such a lovely name. How unfortunate to die so close to Easter."

Marjorie's voice trailed away as Waverley coughed again. Rachel wondered why the surname sounded familiar. The two women waited for him to gather his thoughts, sensing there was a lot more to follow.

"Well, unfortunately it appears Sister Balch may have ingested some sort of toxin that contained digitalis or another substance. We're not quite clear yet. Whatever it was caused her to have some sort of fit, followed by a heart attack. The lab should be sending over a full toxicology report later today, when we'll know for certain what it was. Dr Bentley and the coroner are suggesting it was a digitalis overdose."

"The heart treatment?" Rachel asked.

"From the foxglove plant," added Marjorie.

"Yes, but we don't know for certain. It might turn out to be something other than digitalis that killed her, although Graham Bentley is rarely wrong."

"But why would anyone want to kill a nun?" asked Marjorie.

"Quite," answered Waverley. "Easter Balch, it transpires, may not have been a nun. She changed her name to Easter twelve months ago, and I think she may have been an undercover detective working for the New York Police Department."

Rachel took a sip of tea. "That makes more sense than having a nunophobe on board."

"Is there such a word?" asked Marjorie.

"I don't think so. I just made it up."

"May I continue?" Waverley cut in.

"You may, but I've promised Sarah I'll stay out of your investigation, so you don't need to warn me off or tell me about the dangers of sticking my nose in where it's not welcome."

Waverley coughed again. "Ah, yes, well normally—" he looked at Rachel's father for help.

"Chief Waverley may need your help, Rachel," Brendan said quietly.

Marjorie and Rachel sat up, now paying full attention to what the chief would say next.

"I see," Rachel said.

"Let me explain where we've got to. I have spoken with the Mother Superior of the nunnery. Their holy order is called the Order of the Blue Light."

Rachel nudged Marjorie to stifle a guffaw, knowing that once her friend started laughing, she was unlikely to stop for a while.

"As I was saying," continued Waverley, looking cautiously towards Marjorie, who often managed to get him in a dither, "the Order of the Blue Light is a rather exclusive religious group, but with Catholic leanings. They are funded by a billionaire, and from what I can gather there are small convents scattered around the United States, South America and the Caribbean. They keep themselves separate from society, Mother Cross informs me."

Both women now guffawed and Rachel noticed the corners of her father's mouth turning upwards.

"When you've quite finished, ladies." Waverley couldn't or wouldn't see the joke. "The only thing I find a little odd is that a convent is sent travelling each year, and this year it's the turn of the New York convent."

Marjorie brought herself under control first. "Why are they all so young and beautiful?"

"I asked Mother, erm, Cross that question and she assured me they are not chosen for their looks, something I find difficult to believe. However, the Mother Superior explained that when they do recruit young and beautiful women as trainees, within three months they take a pilgrimage to Brimstone Hill, where the nuns renounce their beauty, cut off their hair, ask for forgiveness and repent of their, erm, attractiveness. They apparently feel instant cleansing and lose all sense of vanity."

Now Marjorie coughed. "Why do they need to ask for forgiveness for the gift they were born with? And why Brimstone Hill?"

"They believe there was a sighting of St Paul on the site of Brimstone Hill Fortress. He reputedly told a young man that he was surrounded by sinful women who flouted their looks. The young man started the movement and called it the Order of the Blue Light because, in his vision, St Paul was covered in blue light. He managed to convince the women of their sinful ways, and later wrote a holy book – an addition to the Bible – to which this particular group adheres. Although Mother, erm, Priscilla – that's her first name – assures me they are not a cult and that Catholicism is the backbone of their beliefs."

"Such stuff and nonsense," said Brendan. "I expect the sighting was in the man's head, and now these poor young women follow a false belief that they should be racked with guilt about God's gift of beauty."

"Dad, I don't think Chief Waverley is a convert. Shall we just hear him out?"

"I agree with your father," said Marjorie, taking another sip of tea. "I take it the sighting is not recognised by the wider Catholic Church?"

"I wouldn't know about that; this is not my area of expertise. In fact, it makes me feel uncomfortable." Waverley looked at Rachel's father for assistance.

"I doubt it is. Sightings have to be numerous, reported by more than one person and over a period of time, as far as

I'm aware, before a site is considered holy. I don't believe Brimstone Hill Fortress is recognised as such. Quite the opposite, I would have thought, considering it was used by the military. There are many offshoots of the Christian Church, though, not all of which I consider sound."

"Anyway," continued Waverley, clearly not wanting to enter into a theological discussion, "the number thirty-seven appears to be significant in this cleansing process, so they always bring thirty-seven young recruits on the pilgrimage. When I contacted Mother Cross, she was considering cancelling the pilgrimage part of the trip. I would rather they didn't cancel, as I wouldn't want them leaving the ship while there could be a murder investigation going on, but I would prefer not to have to insist they stay on board."

"Does Mother Cross know that the death is suspicious?" asked Brendan.

"She does, but I don't want to alert anyone else in the order until we know what is going on. The other nuns believe it was a tragic death, that's all. I don't know how long I can keep it under wraps, though."

"So now you're saying they're one short," said Marjorie thoughtfully.

"Mother Cross believes that thirty-seven remains a key part of the pilgrimage, although she tells me one of the sisters, Sister Murdoch, is adamant it could go ahead without the usual number."

Rachel gawped at Waverley, shaking her head. "You had better not be thinking what I think you are, because if you are, the answer's no. Absolutely not. Not now. Not ever."

Waverley again glanced towards Rachel's father for support.

"I don't like it, Rachel, but you are the right height and weight, and you are beautiful. Someone in this group could be planning something that Easter found out about and Chief Waverley has convinced me this is the only way to put a stop to it. Many lives could be in danger."

"So what was it Easter Balch was on to?"

"That's just it; nobody knows. The NYPD have not come forward yet to admit she was one of theirs, but the coroner believes she was because of the excessive interest shown by the police. I want to be one step ahead. I think we should assume they got a tip-off that members of the order might be involved in criminal activity. I'm trying to contact the detective who has shown interest in the case, but he's not returning my calls as yet."

"Why do you think that is?" asked Rachel.

"I guess he doesn't want to admit to having placed an undercover police officer aboard the *Coral Queen* without permission. Either that or he's busy. We have to remember that the dying woman's word to your father was Armageddon. Stuff like this fills me with dread, I don't mind admitting."

Rachel acknowledged Waverley was truly concerned. "So you don't want to question them about the death because you want to know what, if any, evidence Easter had discovered. I hadn't thought of it before, but nuns would be able to pass through security with ease, as they would be the least likely criminal suspects. In which case, one of them could be carrying anything."

"Precisely, one or more than one. We don't know how many. I've managed to convince Mother Cross to go along with our plan for now, if you agree to infiltrate the order. She's not happy about it, but she will persuade the nuns that Reverend Prince had mentioned in passing how his daughter had a desire to become a nun. She will convince them – because they already know your father is a vicar – that she has offered to give you a trial and take you on as a noviciate."

Marjorie placed her teacup heavily back on to its saucer. "Let me get this straight, Chief Waverley. You want Rachel to go undercover as a nun on the assumption that Easter was a policewoman. An assumption that you have been unable to verify, and that might isolate her and put her in real danger." Marjorie's voice sounded croaky.

"That's about the sum of it," replied Waverley.

"Before you congratulate yourself on this ridiculous plan, don't you think it sounds too convenient? If they are up to something, they will be suspicious," added Marjorie sceptically. "I don't like it at all."

"Convenient to us is divine intervention to those with faith leanings," interjected Brendan. "We just have to convince them to see it from that perspective."

"Dad!" Rachel was shocked. "I never knew you could be so devious. I hope you do believe in divine intervention."

"Of course I do." Brendan winked. "Isn't that why we're here on this particular cruise in a position to stop any further evil being unleashed?"

"I don't know. It sounds complicated, and as Marjorie says, we don't even know if Easter was a police officer. The detective you speak of could have another reason for his interest. Also, I've never worked undercover – apart from a brief episode as a would-be counsellor." She gave Waverley a scathing look. "And I've never been closeted. I'm a Christian, so that part would be easy enough, but what do I know about being a nun? I don't know anything about Catholic rituals."

"You'll also need to remove the engagement ring, my dear," said Marjorie.

Rachel looked down at the ring finger of her left hand and sighed heavily, feeling under pressure.

"What about Mum?"

"Your mother must not know under any circumstances. She would forbid it, and the worry would make her ill. I'll be worried enough for both of us, mind." Rachel's father leaned over and kissed her head. "Somehow we will keep it from her."

"I will keep trying to contact Detective Rodrigues, and if it turns out Easter wasn't a policewoman, you won't be called upon. If she was, we can get you in and out very quickly, but this is one way of stopping them cancelling the pilgrimage. If they try to leave, I will have to question them officially and they will likely clam up."

Rachel sighed, looking at her father. "I don't know how you're going to keep it from Mum."

"Leave that to me. It does mean you won't be able to join us for our rainforest outing in San Juan tomorrow. You'll have to feign a headache or something. Dinner this evening you'll spend with us, as the chief will be arranging for you to join the order from tomorrow morning, if he's right about his assumption."

"Yes, you'll need to behave reverently around the nuns if you come across them, and I'll take you to meet Mother Cross once I've heard from Rodrigues. From tomorrow, you'll be on your own and will need to contact us in whatever way you can. We can't risk a bug, as you'll be sharing a room and we don't know if your roommate is involved."

"Marjorie and I will be seeing the nuns later, as quite a few of them are in the art class. You do realise the killer will be suspicious?" said Rachel.

Waverley coughed. "If you feel like you're in any danger, you must come out immediately. Meanwhile, try to convince everyone you are who Mother Cross says you are and use your skills to dig a little."

"Skills that got a young woman killed, you mean?" said Marjorie. "I don't like this plan one little bit, Chief Waverley. We have no idea what we are up against, and look how easy it was for the poor woman to meet her end."

"Our only advantage is that Rachel fits the bill in every way, and she doesn't have to pretend to be religious. Also we know there could be a killer among them who will be on high alert. Rachel can keep herself out of harm's way as long as she is alert to danger. If I find out later that Easter Balch was not a police officer, you'll be the first to know."

"Who's the roommate?"

"A young woman called Cheryl Sage. She's twenty-seven and Canadian. Here's a photo."

"No need, we've met. She's in our art class. Will Sarah know about this undercover plan?"

"Both she and Doctor Bentley will be informed in case of any mishap. Hopefully the lab will let us know exactly what was used to kill Easter. Graham says digitalis overdose is treatable, and if the murderer tries again, we do have the new intensive care unit." Waverley smiled wryly.

"Not reassuring, Chief. Not reassuring at all," said Rachel.

Chapter 9

Just as Waverley was about to leave Marjorie asked, "Why does the name Balch sound familiar?"

Rachel slapped her own head.

"Of course! Gloria Franks. Dad, I forgot to ask Sarah last night – have you spoken with the Franks yet?"

"No. Your mother told me to ask you this morning – she phoned Mrs Franks last night to tell her the young woman's first name, but said that we would find out the surname just to be certain."

"Will someone tell me what's going on?" Waverley raised his voice.

"We met a woman after the church service yesterday who thought that the collapsed girl was her daughter," said Marjorie. "It appears that mother and daughter had fallen out a few years ago and were estranged. She asked Mrs Prince to find out the name of the girl, who she assumed had fainted. Alas, the daughter's name was Balch – Jacintha Balch."

Waverley paled. "I don't believe this. Jacintha was Easter's name before she changed it. And that's why we haven't found the next of kin. She had listed an uncle, but the number doesn't exist."

"I feel terrible about this," said Brendan. "Would you like us to speak to Mrs Franks? Her daughter had no time for the second husband, according to Susan."

"I do think it would be better coming from you and your wife. Take Rachel with you, and Dr Bentley. I'll let him know. I suggest we keep the cause of death vague for now."

"I was hoping it wouldn't be Mrs Franks's daughter," said Rachel. "But you might need to add Connor Franks to your suspect list. Easter thought he was a gold digger."

"So it might not be some sinister conspiracy after all, Chief," said Marjorie triumphantly.

After Waverley left, the two women accompanied Brendan to the library, where they left him to do crosswords until Susan got back from the hairdresser's.

"What was that about an intensive care unit on board?" Marjorie asked as they exited the room.

"It's something Sarah mentioned when I spoke to her on the phone a few weeks ago. Queen Cruises has decided to add two-bedded intensive care units to the larger ships in the fleet. It means they will be able to ventilate people who are in need of it when they are too far away for swift evacuation. They did have an outdated ventilator before, according to Sarah, but they had to manage people in the infirmary, which wasn't always practical."

"Well if I keel over, just leave it to nature, please. At my age I'd rather make a dignified exit than be attached to tubes and whatnot."

Rachel decided not to argue the point, knowing that Marjorie was strong-minded and well able to make such choices for herself. Instead, she took her friend's arm.

"You're as strong as a truck, so I don't think there is any likelihood of you needing to pay the unit a visit. I don't want to familiarise myself with the place either. I've spent enough time in the infirmary on this ship. Intensive care would be taking it too far. So, what do you really think of this undercover business?"

"Waverley has clearly lost his head is what I think. It feels dangerous. Not only does he not know whether the death was murder – it could have been an accident – he doesn't even know whether Easter Balch worked for the police. I do feel sorry for poor Gloria, though. Let's have another quick cup of tea and then get back to your father."

Rachel sighed. "I do hope Waverley is wrong, because posing as a nun is not my idea of a holiday at all. I'm now more worried about becoming a blue penguin than I am about meeting a potential killer."

Both women laughed, but Rachel was serious. She really wouldn't know where to begin when it came to living in a religious order; she had no experience or insight of what would be expected in a situation like this.

After a refreshing cup of tea and a large slab of cake each in Creams, Rachel and Marjorie found Rachel's parents waiting for them in the library.

"Oh, Rachel, I feel terrible about this. I as good as told Gloria that the woman who died wasn't her daughter."

"She knows Easter's dead then?"

Susan dropped her head. "Yes. He asked if the woman had recovered and I said no, she had died."

"He?" quizzed Marjorie.

"Connor Franks. He answered the phone and said he'd relay the message. I told him I would find out the surname just in case, but he said Gloria would be thrilled it wasn't her daughter."

"You told me you spoke to Gloria." Brendan looked confused.

"Did I? I thought I said I'd let Gloria know the young woman's name. I assumed by telling her husband that was what I was doing."

Rachel's mother could be frustratingly scatty at times, and this was one of those occasions. There hadn't been much genuine concern from Connor Franks, who Rachel was still convinced was after Gloria's money.

"Never mind, I think we should get on with this. I called Dr Bentley before meeting you, he's going to meet us by midships lifts on deck seven."

Dr Bentley was punctual and waiting for them when they arrived. He always made Rachel feel at ease; she supposed it was his calm efficiency in any crisis. He was handsome for a man around her father's age, perhaps a bit older, and he was in good shape.

"I've spoken to the husband. They know we are coming, so at least that's prepared the groundwork," he said.

Rachel introduced her parents, and after a few pleasantries, they headed towards the Franks' room. Marjorie had decided to join them, as she was the one Gloria had first opened up to, and even Connor seemed drawn to the older woman, which might be useful.

Connor opened the door and let them in. Gloria was pacing the floor, wringing her hands, her eyes wide and wild. Rachel's mother immediately crossed the room and drew the already sobbing woman into a warm embrace.

"No, please, no," cried Gloria.

"I'm so sorry," Susan replied.

"What happened?" asked Connor. "I thought the dead woman's name was Easter."

"It was. Shall we sit down?" Dr Bentley suggested.

Gloria almost fell on to the settee and Susan sat beside her, holding her hand. Rachel and Marjorie took the two easy chairs and Dr Bentley sat on the dressing table chair. Connor knelt beside his wife, while Brendan stayed standing.

"It seems the woman known as Easter Balch changed her name a year ago from Jacintha. I understand she was your daughter, Mrs Franks?" Dr Bentley continued.

Gloria nodded, tears flowing down her face. Rachel handed her a box of tissues.

"I'm sorry to inform you that your daughter died yesterday following an overdose of tablets."

"Suicide?" asked Connor.

"Our security team hasn't confirmed that. From what we have gathered, she was happy and there was no suicide note.

The chief of security has spoken to the Mother Superior, who has assured him the Easter she knew was not suicidal."

"An accident, then?" Gloria asked.

"It could have been. I'm sure the chief will want to speak with you sometime today to ask a few questions."

"You're not suggesting she was murdered?" Connor spoke abruptly.

"I'm suggesting that Easter – Jacintha as you knew her, Mrs Franks – died of an overdose of the drug digitalis, and our security team will not be satisfied until they have managed to rule out foul play."

"What's digitalis?" asked Connor.

"It's a heart medication, but it can be poisonous if taken in high doses or by people who don't need it."

"Can you think of anyone who would want to do your daughter harm?" asked Rachel, drawing a look of alarm from her mother.

"No, but we haven't been in touch for a while. As I said yesterday, she was angry with me about my divorce and second marriage. I am only here to check she's happy, and now this."

"These things can be difficult for children to accept, whatever their age," said Brendan, looking at Connor.

"She made life difficult wherever she went, always causing trouble," Connor retorted. The bitter tone could have been a result of being judged the wicked stepfather, not that Easter would have seen him in that role. She saw him as a parasite after her mother's money. Rachel wondered who had stood to inherit before her death – Connor or Easter.

Noticing Gloria becoming more agitated, Brendan asked, "You've had a shock. Do you think a little Valium might help settle the nerves?" He looked questioningly towards Dr Bentley.

Gloria burst into tears again.

"I'm truly sorry for your loss," said Dr Bentley kindly. "I'll give you a prescription and we can get some diazepam sent up from the surgery, if you would like some."

"What's Valium and diazepam?" asked Connor.

"One and the same. One's a trade name used in the UK. The drug is a sedative and will help calm your wife's nerves if needed. Now, I will leave you. I've intruded long enough."

"Would you stay?" Gloria asked Susan as Dr Bentley left the room.

"You go on, Rachel, Marjorie. We'll see you at dinner," said Brendan.

Exchanging sad glances, Marjorie and Rachel silently followed Dr Bentley.

Chapter 10

Dr Bentley left Rachel and Marjorie at the lifts and headed down the stairs.

"Come on, let's grab a bite to eat. One can always think better with food inside. Are we meeting Sarah for lunch?" asked Marjorie.

"I'm not sure. Let's go to the main restaurant. I've just remembered that man and the note."

"Ah well, at least that's a start. Perhaps I should keep watching him after you go undercover," said Marjorie, appearing to be warming to the prospect of getting involved.

"Please be careful if I have to go, Marjorie. I couldn't bear it if anything happened to you."

"Or I you, Rachel. I can't believe that wretched man doesn't feel you should be wearing a wire. It's not right, sending you in blind."

"I've been thinking about that too. It sounds like the overdose was digitalis, from what Dr Bentley said. Perhaps I could ask Waverley if he has any new state of the art equipment."

"Now that is more like it. I saw a film where a woman wore a camera brooch."

"Marjorie, I don't think nuns wear brooches!"

"Oh. Perhaps they could hide a tape recorder in a Bible or something."

"Now you're talking," said Rachel, squeezing her friend's arm. "A modern day equivalent at least. I think the whole undercover police thing sounds too far-fetched anyway. It's more likely to be a good old-fashioned case of envy, jealousy or greed."

"I would add sex, but that wouldn't fit, would it?"

"Easter could have a past that's caught up with her. We know she wasn't always going to be a nun, that she had dubious friends. What did her mother say? 'The wrong sort of people'."

"That could mean anything coming from a parent."

"You're right, but her death might not be linked to her job at all, even if she was a police officer. It could be some ex-criminal who has it in for her or any number of other things. The death could also be related to her mother's wealth in some way, and that would put Connor Franks in the frame."

"Or it might be one of the nuns. We can't rule them out. We've witnessed how unpleasant they can be to each other for ourselves."

"I agree, we can't rule them out."

The restaurant was busy, but not full. Rachel was pleased to see the man in her sights at the same table where he'd sat the previous evening.

"Looks just as miserable as he did last night," whispered Marjorie.

Rachel didn't reply as a waiter appeared to attend to them. Marjorie scanned the menu.

"I think I'll try a Jamaican jerk chicken open sandwich, please. Orange juice to drink, thank you."

"Yes, ma'am, good choice. And for you, Miss?"

Rachel wasn't hungry. Her stomach was in knots at the prospect of spending the remainder of her cruise dressed as a nun, and the piece of cake from earlier was still sitting heavily.

"Olive salad and tonic water, please."

Marjorie winked after the waiter had left. "You'll be fine, you know. Once you've infiltrated them, your police genes will kick in and you'll improvise."

Rachel smiled at her elderly friend, but the knot in her stomach wouldn't go away. "I hope you're right, Marjorie, because this has to be the most frightening assignment of my life—"

"LOOK WHAT YOU'RE DOING, MAN!"

Their conversation was interrupted by bellowing from the man they had come to observe. A fellow passenger had knocked into his table when a freak wave caused him to stumble.

"I'm so sorry; I lost my balance for a moment. Here, let me help you with that." The passenger attempted to stoop down to pick up the man's mobile phone.

"Get off!" The spindly man slapped the passenger's hand away as he grabbed the phone. Rachel simultaneously threw her serviette to the floor and bent down to pick it up, giving her just enough time to notice the end of a text.

"All clear, proceed as planned."

The rude man was too busy fending off the maître d to notice her.

"Mr Cooper, sir, you're making a scene. Is there anything I can do to help?"

The other passenger walked away, muttering about ignorant people.

Cooper stood up, having pocketed the phone. "No thanks, Colin; it was a misunderstanding. Fellow damn near broke my phone."

With the hubbub over, passengers resumed their meals.

"Well, isn't he a nasty piece of stuck-up mutton?"

"He certainly is. But we now know at least two things about him."

"Before you share them, what did you see on the phone? I suspect your napkin didn't fall accidentally."

"A text." Rachel relayed the message. "It could have been an appointment in the spa, for all we know."

"Or it could be referring to the death of Easter Balch," said Marjorie.

"You would make a great detective, Marjorie. What his behaviour tells us – apart from the obvious, that he runs on a short fuse – is that we need to ask Waverley to look into his background."

"What are the two things we now know?"

"His name's Cooper and he cruises regularly."

"What makes you say he's a regular cruiser?"

"He knew Colin Bell's first name and felt able to use it."

"You're right. I've known Colin for many years, having sailed regularly myself, but I would never have called him by his first name until Ralph and I were invited to do so after being awarded platinum membership. You don't think Colin could be mixed up with our crime in some way, do you?"

Rachel had been wondering about that herself, having noticed the maître d seeming to flash a warning look towards the man named Cooper.

"I hope not, I like Colin Bell. Did you notice the emphasis on Mister, though? It was almost sarcastic."

"I did, actually. Most unusual to see Colin growling at a passenger, particularly – if what we suspect is right – a platinum passenger."

"We need to pass on this information to Waverley. Let's go back to your suite and call him. I don't want to be seen near his office, as I'm going to need to keep a low profile. Did you notice whether that man Cooper was in the theatre for the church service yesterday?"

"Sorry, no. I wasn't really taking much notice. My attention was on your father and the Blue Lights."

Rachel giggled. "Blue light to me means get there fast in a cop car."

"There you are, then, you'll feel right at home within the Order of the Blues and Twos."

Chapter 11

Marjorie let Waverley into her suite and motioned for him to take a seat. Coffee had been delivered by Mario moments before and Marjorie set about pouring them each a cup. Waverley knew better than to interrupt Lady Snellthorpe before she was sitting comfortably with a drink in her hand, but Rachel noticed he was tense.

She broke the silence. "We wanted to let you know there's been a development that might be something or nothing, I'm not quite sure which."

Waverley sat forward in his chair and took a gulp of coffee, giving the impression he hadn't had much time to drink since their meeting this morning.

"Go on," he prompted.

"We had the misfortune of coming across an unpleasant – well, downright rude – man last night in the Coral Restaurant. He was impolite to a passenger and inadvertently to my mother, which is why he drew my attention. While watching him, I noticed he may have passed a note to one of the nuns as a crowd of them left the room."

"Did you see which one?"

"The one dressed in blue." Rachel smiled and Marjorie chuckled at the joke.

Waverley tensed even more. "I take it from that you don't know who?"

"To be honest, no, and I'm not even sure of what I witnessed. It was one of those situations where you think you've seen something, but when thinking back later, you're not certain. Do you know what I mean?"

"Can't say I do." Waverley's reply was terse and he squeezed the bridge of his nose.

"Well I certainly do, Rachel. There are so many occasions these days when I think I've remembered something, but if I had to swear to it, I don't think I could. Just the other day—"

"I'm sorry, Lady Snellthorpe, but do you think we could get back to my reason for being here? I have a meeting in ten minutes."

"Tell me later," said Rachel, smiling at her friend. Marjorie smiled back appreciatively, but glared at Waverley.

"Today, after visiting Gloria and Connor Franks – I think you need to look into Connor, by the way – Marjorie and I decided to go to the Coral Restaurant to see if the bad-mannered man was there again. I wanted to check if he behaved suspiciously."

"And did he?"

Ignoring the question, Rachel continued, "He was alone this time – his wife was with him last night – but he was just as foul as he had been yesterday. A poor man had the misfortune of bumping into his table and knocked his mobile phone out of his hand. While he was picking it up, I managed to read a text arriving on the screen. The only other things we noticed were that his name is Cooper and he is on first name terms with Colin Bell."

"You're not suggesting that Colin—"

"We're not suggesting anything, Chief, other than Cooper may be involved in something that is going on with these nuns," said Marjorie.

"What did the text say?"

Rachel told him what she had read on Cooper's phone.

"That could mean anything. I don't see this has anything to do with the case. Is there anything else, other than you think I should look into Connor Franks for some reason?" The redness from Waverley's neck extended to his face.

"Chief, I think you should at least look into this man Cooper and find out who he is and what he's doing on board this ship. Unless, of course, you would like us to do that for you as well as everything else." Marjorie was losing patience with the chief of security. They had an up-and-down relationship and Marjorie could give him quite a hard time when she put her mind to it. "Perhaps he's a relative of yours, judging by present behaviour," she muttered.

"Okay, I'll look him and Franks up, but I think we're wasting our time here. We have enough to do as it is trying to find a murderer."

"Well Connor Franks could have a motive for murder for one thing. He's Gloria's gigolo husband and Rachel believes he may have a past and be after the woman's wealth."

"Well, if Rachel believes it, it must be true," Waverley snapped, startling both women.

Rachel knew that Waverley could be defensive when under pressure, so she replied gently, "Well that's all we have for now."

Waverley stood to leave. "Ladies." He nodded as he headed towards the door. Marjorie escorted him and called after him as he was about to walk away.

"Chief?"

He turned. "Yes?"

"You asked Rachel to get involved in this case and I would remind you that you may be putting her in danger. The least you can do is show some respect to her, and to me, when we have something to share."

Waverley was left open-mouthed as Marjorie closed the door.

"What the heck is wrong with him? It's like dealing with Jekyll and Hyde at times."

"He was a bit off, wasn't he? I guess he's got a lot on his mind."

"Indeed, and just as I was warming to him."

"His loss. I'll give Sarah a call and arrange to meet up with her and Jason after dinner. Perhaps Jason will be more helpful."

"That's a great idea. Jason is such an even-headed young man, not at all like his boss."

Rachel got up. She was also annoyed with Waverley, but didn't want Marjorie to be any more fired up than she already was.

"Come on, we'd better get to our art lesson and see if there's anything else we can unearth between now and tomorrow morning."

Rachel and Marjorie found places on the same table with four of the five nuns from the day before, and they each stuck rigidly to their previous seats. Only Sister Murdoch wasn't at their table; Rachel noticed she had joined another table, where a few of the younger nuns had been giggling the day before.

"Ah, no leader today," said Marjorie pleasantly to Cheryl and Letitia, who both grinned widely.

"I don't know why she sat over there. She was sitting next to me, and then moved," complained Blethyn, again sitting beside Rachel.

"There, there. Mummy will be back soon, I'm sure," teased Letitia. Cheryl giggled, but stopped when she noticed Blethyn glaring. Rachel noticed tears welling up in the overly serious woman's eyes.

"Sorry," said Letitia.

"So you should be. You know how Blethyn dotes on Sister Murdoch," said Angeline.

Rachel felt a nudge in her ribs from Marjorie. It wouldn't be unusual for young, impressionable women to form an attachment to an older woman in authority, but it was odd that it seemed to be Sister Murdoch who attracted the most respect and, in Cheryl's case at least, fear. Mother Cross hadn't been mentioned.

There was no way she could join this order as an undercover noviciate. Her acting skills were just not up to the task. She would let Waverley know later that it wasn't going to happen.

Besides, she remembered, I've been wearing my engagement ring and I'm sure one of them will have noticed.

"Are you all on holiday?" Rachel asked Letitia, who today, without Sister Murdoch present, seemed to be the most open of the group. Blethyn and Angeline had plenty of confidence, but were more guarded.

"We're on a pilgrimage."

"Oh, how exciting," said Marjorie. "I didn't realise any of the stops on this cruise were of particular religious significance."

"They're not to most Catholics," said Angeline fiercely.

"Unless you're in the know," added Blethyn.

"What do you mean?" asked Rachel, turning to Blethyn.

"Our order has knowledge of sightings that aren't mainstream because we are particularly blessed. St Paul will only reveal himself to those who are truly sincere and ardent in their beliefs. He revealed himself to Monsignor Raucous, who founded our order."

Rachel nudged Marjorie before she could say anything about the name Raucous, having to prevent the corners of her own mouth from turning upwards.

"I see. Well obviously I don't see, but where have these sightings taken place?"

"We're not exactly sure," admitted Angeline. "But somewhere near Brimstone Hill Fortress on St Kitts."

"Oh really? I thought that was a military establishment. Didn't your father say that, Rachel?"

"Yes, he did."

"He's a vicar, you know," Marjorie added.

"Oh, was he the vicar who led the service yesterday morning and tried to help...?" Cheryl's voice trailed off.

"I apologise, I remember now – a young woman in your order was taken seriously ill, wasn't she? How insensitive of me. I believe she died," said Marjorie. "What a tragedy. I expect you're all quite upset about it."

Rachel watched the reactions around the table carefully. Blethyn and Angeline exchanged glances, Letitia looked down at her artwork, and Cheryl's head swung round to make sure Sister Murdoch hadn't heard anything. It was peculiar.

"It was awful. I was sitting next to her when it happened," said Cheryl, satisfied the older nun was busy with the charges on the other table. "We shared a room."

"They didn't get on, though," Blethyn sneered.

"We did, too!" Cheryl protested.

"Leave her," Letitia snarled at Blethyn, who shrugged.

Angeline remained quiet and Rachel felt the woman's eyes boring into her. Suspicions aroused or just an angry young woman? Rachel wasn't sure which.

"It must be hard to lose one of your own in such tragic circumstances. My father was upset, having witnessed the whole thing."

The conversation was interrupted by Dwaine, who felt it was time to bring the class back to order so that he could move them on from the still life paintings. After a short lesson in watercolours, he told them to add something to their work from their own imagination.

Rachel looked down at her pathetic attempt at fruit and realised that art was not going to be one of her callings. Blethyn had already painted a fine piece of work, as had Marjorie. Rachel's friend was keen to pursue the earlier conversation, but Rachel wanted to proceed with caution in case Angeline did suspect they were digging.

"How did you decide that being nuns was right for you? It's something I've wondered about, but never really understood."

"I joined when I realised how sincere Sister Murdoch was. We met when I was working as a nursing assistant in a hospital in New York," Blethyn volunteered. It was interesting there was no mention of a calling or conversion, Rachel noted.

"Are you from New York?" she asked.

"Originally I'm from Waterford in Ireland. My ancestors were Irish immigrants, so my family moved to New

York when my father transferred. He works for Pfizer, the pharmaceutical company. Anyway, I now have dual nationality – not an easy achievement, but Sister Murdoch says I'm as American as she is. This order has become my life. I will fight anyone who tries to destroy it."

Interesting outburst, thought Rachel. She clearly runs on a short fuse, overly zealous and loyal.

"Why should anyone want to destroy your order?" she asked.

"They don't," snapped Angeline. "Blethyn's just passionate about what we believe and all the good we are doing in the world, aren't you, Bleth?"

"And what about you, dear? What made you become a nun?" Marjorie asked Angeline before she could shut down the conversation altogether.

"I admire Mother Cross. Everything about her is holy. I want to be like her in every way. One day I'll be a Mother Superior and lead a convent of devotees."

"Whoa, hold on a minute, you're not even a proper nun yet," said Letitia, laughing. "Angeline can get above herself sometimes. Comes from being brought up in an orphanage, doesn't it? She's read too many stories about rags to riches."

"Well I hardly think being a nun demonstrates that type of ambition. There's nothing wrong with wanting to lead people," said Marjorie protectively.

This drew a grin from Angeline. "Exactly. Mother Cross says I have all the makings of being a great nun. At least she did until—"

"Until what, dear?" asked Marjorie.

Angeline looked down at her painting, sulking. "Nothing. I'm going to the toilet." She left the table.

"She got a bit jealous of Easter, our dead sister. Mother Cross would have private meetings with her when no-one else was around. Angeline found out about them and felt she was being usurped." Cheryl lowered her voice to a whisper. "Truth be told, I think she's pleased Easter's no longer with us."

"Don't be ridiculous," said Letitia. "She wouldn't want her dead."

"I'm not saying that, I'm just saying she wasn't unhappy to hear she wasn't coming back, that's all."

Cheryl looked anxious again. The nuns fell silent and continued their painting. Rachel stared at her own rather feeble effort, deep in thought.

Chapter 12

Dinner that evening was in the Coral
Restaurant and Rachel's father
entertained the company with stories of
his years as a parish vicar in the village
where Rachel had grown up. He had
many tales of parishioners' antics, all told
in good humour, and Marjorie and he
were getting along well, which pleased
Rachel. Her friend had just as many
stories of her own exploits – Marjorie had
entertained the rich and famous due to her
husband's business dealings over six
decades.

"Who was the most famous person you
met?" asked Susan.

"I met many famous people, but the nicest, and the most precious to Ralph and me, was the Queen. People think she's stuffy, but she's not, you know. She has a wicked sense of humour."

"So I've heard," said Brendan.

"I did meet many so-called celebrities who dabbled with business. Not all pleasant, I can tell you. I also met some of the richest people in the world, but most of them you wouldn't recognise if you passed them in the street. Some of these men and women donate huge sums back into society through philanthropy, but no-one knows it except the charities they support because they don't advertise it – unlike many of our celebrities today."

Rachel could have listened to the stories all night long. Both her father and Marjorie were able to hold an audience with engaging narrative and sharp wit.

She would be glad to be like either of them when she was older.

Her attention had been on the man she now knew as Cooper in the early part of the evening, but she was soon drawn away from any interest in him to enjoy the company she was with. Her mother looked happier this evening. The shock of young Easter Balch's death the previous day had weighed heavily, and Susan and Brendan had spent a fair part of the morning with Gloria and Connor Franks. They'd even had lunch together. Susan had told Rachel she'd found it traumatic, as Gloria was understandably devastated about losing her estranged daughter. When Rachel asked about Connor's behaviour, her mother had tutted and told her she wasn't on duty, but Susan now appeared to be relaxing into her holiday. She looked beautiful this evening and her face was radiant. The olive cocktail dress hugged her in all the right places and she was clearly enjoying the opportunity to dress up and pamper herself.

The lot of a vicar's wife is often one of serving the community, attending committee meetings and raising money for good causes, all of which Susan Prince did with aplomb, but it was good to see her in a different light. Rachel was determined that her parents' holiday would not be ruined by criminals.

"Are you two young women going anywhere after dinner?" Brendan asked, winking at Marjorie and sipping a glass of brandy.

"Yes, we're going to meet Sarah and Jason in the Jazz Bar once Sarah's surgery is finished. Do you want to come?"

"No thank you. Your mother's tired after all the day's activities and the fresh sea air."

Susan appeared far from tired, but was happy to take the hint that Rachel and Marjorie might want to meet Sarah and Jason without them tagging along.

"I do wish you wouldn't answer for me, Brendan. You know it will only get you into trouble." Turning to Rachel, Susan continued, "We are going to the evening show, but obviously your father has no memory for our plans."

"The show! Sorry, Susan, I forgot. Yes, we're going to the theatre. I can't keep up with all this entertainment. You did warn me, Rachel, but I thought you had to be exaggerating."

Rachel kissed her parents goodnight and took Marjorie's arm, heading towards the Jazz Bar.

"Cooper was quiet tonight, wasn't he?" Marjorie said once they were out of earshot.

"He was. Perhaps his wife has told him off." Rachel was now pondering what, if anything, he had to do with the death of Easter Balch. She also felt they were nowhere near finding out who'd killed the poor woman and was concerned that any involvement might endanger Marjorie, and the unsuspecting Susan.

Marjorie patted Rachel's hand. "Perhaps Jason can help us with our investigation."

"Marjorie Snellthorpe! It's their investigation and there's no 'our' about it."

"Humph. Well someone has to look out for you if you're going undercover, as clearly the chief of security can't to be relied upon to do so. Officious man!"

Before Rachel had the opportunity to explain she wasn't going undercover, Marjorie was accosted by an excited quartet sitting in a booth away from the busiest part of the Jazz Bar. Sarah and Jason were there, accompanied by Brigitte and Bernard.

The small nurse hugged Rachel again. "Beautiful as ever. I don't know how it is that you can get more good-looking each time we meet – and that's just you, Lady Snellthorpe."

"I've already warned you – I'm Marjorie to you, and watch your cheek, young man." Marjorie grinned back at Bernard. His wide smile was infectious, as was his humour.

"I have said it before and I'll say it again – I knew as soon as you two were on board there would be a murder." He couldn't resist another quip as they each took seats in the booth. "Although I have to say, I'm not happy with the murder of a nun."

"She probably wasn't a nun, you dumbhead," said Brigitte. "You men are useless when it comes to facts."

Rachel was happy to be in the company of Sarah and her friends. Bernard was full of energy and could not resist mischief making, even more so when the serious Brigitte was around, because he knew it drove her to distraction. And she could never resist bringing up her opinion on the shortfalls of the male species.

"And you, my little French nettle, are the most sexist person I have ever worked with." Bernard folded his arms in defiance.

"Who are you calling little? I'm two inches taller than you."

Sarah laughed. "Now, now, you two. Come on or I'll have to ask Jason to send you both to bed without supper."

"Good to see you, Rachel," said Jason. "And you, Lady… erm, Marjorie."

"We're pleased to be here, aren't we, Rachel? Let me buy everyone a drink, and then we can talk."

Jason called a waiter over and ordered a tonic water, as he didn't drink alcohol. Sarah, who was still carrying the on-call bag, ordered lemonade. Rachel had her usual martini and lemonade, Marjorie brandy, Bernard a Scotch, while Brigitte requested a Pernod and blackcurrant. Once the drinks were on the table, they chatted amicably for a while before moving on to the death of Easter Balch again.

"The chief's not happy because he's been told by the powers that be to stay away from the nuns. We've basically been ordered off the case and they won't give us any further information. Just saying it's now an FBI investigation. The NYPD are livid as well, according to the boss. Some detective over there wants to make sure that someone's brought to account for the death of the woman, but no-one will say whether she was genuinely a nun or an undercover cop. It's a mess. Waverley's told me to let you know that you're off the case, too, Rachel. No undercover work required."

"Well I can't say I'm sorry to hear that," said Marjorie. "It was a foolhardy idea in the first place, and far too dangerous."

"I agree," said Sarah, who would not have approved of any plan leading to the remotest chance of her best friend coming to any harm.

Rachel was thoughtful. At least she didn't have to tell her friends she'd decided not to go undercover, but she didn't want to abandon the investigation while it was still warm.

"Why have the FBI got involved with it? And what about international maritime rules and all that?" she asked.

"We're in US waters, and the cruise line is American, so they're happy to hand it over. Not interested, Waverley says. As for the why, they're not even telling the boss, and you can imagine how much that's riling him." Jason took a drink from his glass.

"Well, I say leave them to it," said Brigitte. "You know I don't like murderers going around on—"

"MY SHIP!" they all chimed in, anticipating Brigitte's next words.

"Exactly," she said, joining in the laughter.

"I'm inclined to agree," said Marjorie. "I didn't like the thought of you being out of contact anyway, Rachel. The chief should never have asked you to go undercover in my opinion."

Bernard grinned across the table at Rachel. "Undercover or no, she will not leave this alone, will you, DS Prince?"

"Oh, I forgot to say congratulations," said Jason.

"Thanks."

"When do you start?" he asked, giving Bernard a warning look to say no more.

"As soon as we get back. Marjorie's kindly arranged for her chauffeur to move my stuff up to my new place while we're away. I'll spend a night with my parents when we get back to England, and then move up to Leicester ready to start on the Monday."

"What about Carlos?" asked Jason.

"He travels a lot anyway, so it won't make a huge difference to our seeing each other. He's keeping his office in London. We've also set a date for the wedding."

Cheers and laughter spread through the group after what had been a sombre day. They all congratulated Rachel.

"As many of you that can come are invited. We've arranged for the service to be held on a Saturday when the *Coral* is in port, and even if you can't make it, you'll see us later that day because we are having our reception and honeymoon on board ship."

"That's wonderful news, Rachel," said Bernard. "Will your father be marrying you?"

"Yep! We debated getting married on board where we first met, but decided instead to do a repeat of the Mediterranean cruise for the honeymoon – without the murder."

"And without any distraction from me," added Marjorie, who still baulked at the memory of that particular cruise. "Not my fondest holiday, but it did have a positive side. I made some dear friends."

The group nodded understanding, and then wanted to know all the finer details. Sarah had known the couple had set the date; she was delighted that Rachel and Carlos would be having a honeymoon on board the *Coral Queen* so she would get to see them for longer after the wedding as she wasn't due a break until the autumn.

"I have invitations from my parents to give out to the medical team. I'll let you have them tomorrow."

"Sounds perfect," said Bernard. "It will make a change for me not to be the only one married in our little group. Although I don't think others will be long behind."

Rachel gawped at Sarah and Jason.

"Not us; we've not set a date yet, but Alex has got engaged and will be getting married in Rome in the autumn."

"Except the downside is, he's leaving us," said Brigitte.

"Oh?"

"Yes, he's going to take his new bride home to Rome and work in his father's practice. There's a shortage of doctors over there now and he wants to get back to normality, he says. He travelled with Medicine Sans Frontieres and worked in refugee camps before he joined this ship. I think he wants to settle down in one place for a while."

Alex was the junior doctor on board the *Coral Queen* and someone Rachel had got to know in his professional capacity as a medic. His main priority was taking care of the health of crew members, but he was called upon to see passengers at other times when Dr Bentley was busy elsewhere or on shore leave.

"The end of an era," Brigitte sighed. "What's worse is we will have to get used to a new baby doc. We've just got Alex trained to our way of working."

The term 'baby doc' was used to refer to junior doctors on board a cruise ship and Rachel always smiled at it. The medical team mostly referred to Alex Romano as Alex now because he'd been with them for years, but any new doctor would have to put up with the reference for a while. Rachel understood the anxiety Brigitte was talking about as the medical team worked under constant pressure and in close contact, so it was vital they all got on.

"I bet Dr Bentley will miss him," she said.

"On that note, we think there's another budding romance in the medical centre, too," whispered Bernard.

"You don't know anything. Stop spreading rumours," chastised Brigitte.

"I know what I know, my nose detects things. Rachel sniffs out murderers, I can sniff romance from miles away."

"Oh, do tell. I like a bit of gossip," encouraged Marjorie.

"Graham and Gwen," he said triumphantly.

"What's that, Bernard?" The senior nurse, Gwen Sumner, appeared behind Bernard before Rachel got the chance to warn him. Bernard's face reddened as he scrunched his forehead.

Marjorie came to the rescue. "Bernard was just saying how you and Dr Bentley will be delighted with Rachel's news."

"What news?" The Australian nurse sat down.

"We've set a date for the wedding in the summer. You're all invited, and Carlos and I will be joining the *Coral Queen* for our honeymoon."

"Now that is good news. We could do with some." Gwen frowned towards Bernard, not totally convinced by Marjorie's intervention. Bernard mouthed his thanks to Marjorie as Rachel recounted all she had just said to the others before Gwen's arrival. The happy bunch appeared not to have a care in the world. No-one watching them would have suspected that, for some of them at least, murder, not weddings, had been at the front of their minds only hours earlier.

Chapter 13

The morning sun trickled through a gap in the heavy drapes in Rachel's room. She knew it was early, but got out of bed anyway and pulled open the curtains. The view was spectacular, despite the ship being docked. High-rise buildings filled the foreground and palm trees could be seen in the background. The sky was wonderfully blue. She could hear activity portside as port staff went about their morning work.

As her parents would still be in bed, she decided to take an early morning run around deck sixteen. The sun was already a brilliant orb in the sky, but the temperature was just about bearable at

23°C, according to her new smart watch. It would be much hotter later, so now was a good time to take advantage of the relative quiet.

It was 5.30am when she left the room, and she was soon running circuits around the upper deck in comfort, listening to songs played randomly by her phone through earplugs. She passed a few other early morning runners, mainly crew, but one or two middle-aged passengers were power walking around the deck. She had passed them eight times by the time she stopped.

An idea came to her while she was running and she couldn't shake it off, despite warning bells telling her to go back to her room. The chapel was close by and she was almost certain the nuns would be congregating for morning prayers. Shaking away any doubts, she proceeded in that direction.

On entering the small chapel, she resisted a shout of 'yes', and inwardly congratulated herself on being right instead. Nuns in blue habits were scattered throughout the quiet room, mostly praying silently, although she could hear a few murmurings. Rachel noticed an elderly couple sitting at the back, holding hands and silently praying with their eyes closed. She walked stealthily past them, pleased she was wearing trainers, and positioned herself behind a pillar just big enough to allow her to observe without being obvious unless someone passed that way.

A trio of older nuns, including Sister Murdoch and someone she assumed was Mother Cross, sat on one end of the row furthest away from her. Rachel smiled on recalling the Mother Superior's name. She counted thirty-one others present, but she couldn't see any faces, so was unable to tell who was who.

Rachel sat for fifteen minutes and was about to leave, deciding there was nothing unusual to see other than nuns at prayer, when the door behind her opened. She craned her neck to catch a glimpse of who had entered and was surprised to see Colin Bell accompanied by the unpleasant man, Cooper. She ducked her head back behind the pillar as Cooper glanced quickly around the chapel. The room was relatively dark so he didn't see her – not that she thought he would recognise her even if he did.

Colin parked himself at the back, where the elderly couple had left a short row of chairs empty, while Cooper walked towards the front. Rachel strained to get her head around the pillar to see what he was up to, but struggled as he veered off to the right. Moments later, he moved back to the centre, bowed to the large cross at the front of the chapel, and returned to the rear, exiting without Colin Bell, who remained seated.

Cooper hadn't struck Rachel as remotely religious – not that you could always tell, her father had said on many occasions – so she suspected a different reason for his appearance in the chapel. At least it confirmed that he could be linked to the nuns, not that he'd acknowledged anyone that she could see.

Rachel stayed where she was, trying to see if any of the nuns went in the direction that Cooper had gone, but it was impossible. As the clock struck the half hour to herald 6.30am, most of the nuns gathered together in a gaggle and all she could see was a mass of blue habits. They spoke quietly amongst themselves before making their way out of the chapel, where the noise level increased and could be heard through the partially open door.

Colin Bell had already left, but Rachel hadn't seen when. The older nuns had exited shortly after Cooper. There was now just her and two nuns left seated. The remaining pair clearly thought the chapel was empty, as Rachel could hear their conversation. It changed volume from whispers to raised voices.

"Don't, Cheryl. It could be dangerous and you don't know for certain."

Rachel's ears pricked up – Cheryl had been Easter's roommate.

"I can't stay any longer, Angeline. There's something going on. Easter was up to something. I caught her using a phone in our room. There might be something going on that's illegal."

"Perhaps she was just calling home. Not everyone obeys the rules, you know that. Particularly Easter Balch, she didn't know when to keep her mouth shut. Always asking ridiculous questions. I don't know what Mother Cross saw in her."

There was that same jealousy Angeline had expressed during the art class. Rachel wondered whether there was more to it than petty bickering.

"I can't say I liked her either. We got on okay, but she wasn't my type. Still, I don't think she was calling home. I heard her tell whoever it was she was speaking to that thousands could be affected. Come to think of it now, I don't know whether she said affected or infected."

"Affected, I would think, and there you are, then. She was talking about the pilgrimage and the coming revival that Sister Murdoch talks about."

"Oh! I didn't think of that. But we are forbidden to tell people about that."

"I know, Cheryl, but she was a bit of an odd one. As I say, always asking questions when she wasn't supposed to – I think she was a rebel. Perhaps she got what was coming to her. It was the hand of God."

Rachel swallowed hard, resisting the temptation to leap out of her seat and put this woman to rights. She didn't need to.

"Angeline, you shouldn't say things like that. I'm still shocked she died. Besides, God would never do such a thing! That's a wicked thought."

Rachel noticed Angeline crossing herself. "Sorry, you're right, but there's no denying she was a rebel and didn't fit in. I don't think she would have made it past the noviciate. You've got nothing to worry yourself about."

"I wonder why she asked all those questions, though. It was as if she was trying to find out our secrets. I didn't like that."

"Why? Have you got something to hide, Cheryl Sage?"

"Sisters!" A loud voice came from behind. Rachel noticed Sister Murdoch had changed and was now dressed in black as opposed to the dark grey she'd had on earlier. She had entered quietly through the doors, pale and ghostlike, her large crooked nose making her look more like a witch than a nun. Could that nose have been broken at some stage in her life?

The two nuns leapt up. "Sorry, Sister, we were chatting."

"Idle chatter does not become you. Now off you go, both of you."

As the two nuns headed Rachel's way, she ducked down just in case they did see her and closed her eyes, pretending to be asleep. When she was left in the silence of the chapel, she took the opportunity to pray herself for guidance as to how to get to the bottom of Easter Balch's death. What had Cheryl heard Easter saying? Easter would not have been referring to the pilgrimage or any future revival, of that Rachel was certain.

After a while, she made her way to the front of the chapel and turned right towards the area she had seen Cooper go. There were some torch candles with switches to the side of each one, and some were lit. Perhaps he had been lighting a candle for someone. She had an uncomfortable feeling about Colin Bell being linked to this man Cooper, who she was convinced was involved in something covert.

Having allowed ten minutes for the nuns to be well clear of the chapel, Rachel exited by the main doors. She needed to speak to Waverley at some stage.

After Rachel had showered and dressed, she and Marjorie enjoyed breakfast in Marjorie's suite while her parents went to the buffet.

"What do you think it all means, Rachel?" Marjorie had listened intently to Rachel's account of her spying session in the ship's chapel.

"I don't know, but it could be something to do with the reason that Easter Balch was murdered. Having said that, it might not mean anything at all. Easter could have been the rebel they said she was. She wasn't very popular, though, from what I heard in the chapel. Not that subtle with her questioning, either, and Cheryl appeared to be hiding something that she was worried Easter might have found out. Perhaps she was just trying to dig out dirt in people's lives, or perhaps she was a police officer. I wish we knew one way or another about that, it's frustrating. I don't like feeling we might be making assumptions that have no grounds. Why all the secrecy? Is it something to do with their pilgrimage and the revival, like Angeline suggested, or something more sinister?"

"It's more than likely to be a simple case of jealousy, unless someone among them does have something else to hide. If Easter was asking a lot of questions, other things may have been revealed. The FBI getting involved does suggest something unusual, doesn't it? That rather points to the dead woman being an undercover policewoman. You say, from what you observed, they were genuinely religious?"

"In the conversation I overheard, they seemed earnest in their beliefs. I would like to get to speak to Cheryl alone, though. She seems nervous all the time, anxious and twitching, but I don't know why. We can ask Waverley later for some of the background details."

"Jason might be a better option."

"I don't like to compromise him with his boss. He's loyal and it wouldn't feel right to go around Waverley."

"But we will if we have to."

"Oh yes, we will if we have to. Now, come on, it's time to meet my parents and go ashore. The island looks stunning from what I can see."

Twenty minutes later, Rachel and Marjorie were waiting in the main atrium for Rachel's parents to arrive when they saw Waverley march through before speaking to a purser. He turned and saw them and, after a quick look round, joined them.

"Good morning, ladies. I would like to apologise for my behaviour yesterday. I had a lot on my mind – I suppose Goodridge told you we have been ordered off the case?"

"Yes, but why by the FBI? And did she work for the NYPD or not?" asked Marjorie.

Waverley coughed. "They won't say, but one of them hinted over the phone to the captain that it's about the misappropriation of large sums of money. I'm waiting for two FBI agents to join me now and hopefully they can explain what the heck's going on. They won't say whether Easter Balch was working for them, the NYPD, or neither. It's frustrating. I'm not happy to pull the security team off this at all, but Captain Jenson has ordered me to let it go. I can't go against a direct order." Waverley rubbed the top of his head and held out his other hand helplessly.

"Quite," said Marjorie.

"You're very quiet, Rachel. Don't tell me you still plan to involve yourself."

"Well I can't say I'm disappointed not to be dressed as a blue penguin this morning, but other than that, erm—"

Rachel's parents approached just at the right moment, as Rachel wasn't ready to give an answer to Waverley's question.

"Let's meet up tonight," he suggested.

"My room, six o'clock sharp. We're going ashore for dinner this evening, so we'll need to be succinct," said Marjorie as she stood up to greet Rachel's parents.

Waverley sighed. "Ladies." He got up. "Mr and Mrs Prince, I hope you are enjoying your stay aboard the *Coral Queen*."

"Oh we are, immensely," answered Brendan.

"No Nurse Bradshaw today?" the chief asked.

"She was on call last night. She's joining us this afternoon when she gets off duty," said Rachel.

"Ah, I think the medical team was busy last night." Waverley lowered his voice to a whisper. "Sunburn – it always happens after a few days at sea. People don't realise how harmful the sun's rays are when reflected off the blue waters of the Caribbean – or any other sea for that matter. Thankfully some of them do slap sun cream on the children and the captain makes regular announcements to do so, as you know, and there's always advice in the *Coral News*, but some parents think they're immune."

Rachel looked at her father's skin, bronzed from years spent in his precious garden. Gardening was a hobby that kept him fit and helped him de-stress from the worries of shepherding an unusually large congregation. Her mother's skin was paler and Rachel could see from the shine of exposed areas that she had applied sun cream. She was wearing a sleeveless summer dress and sunhat, but sturdy sandals for the day's walking. Her father carried a boater in his hand.

"No worries here, Chief. Susan is meticulous with its application. As soon as we get off ship, she'll be nagging Rachel to don the stuff. Don't think you'll get away with it either, Marjorie." Brendan's eyes twinkled with pleasure.

"Brendan, you're insufferable sometimes. I'm not like that at all, although you do look like you could do with some cream, Rachel."

Rachel's mouth curled up in response.

"Time to go, I think," said Marjorie, leading the group away from an amused Waverley. "At least we managed to cheer him up," she whispered. "Although strictly speaking, I think San Juan is still in the Atlantic Ocean, not the Caribbean Sea."

"I'm so pleased you resisted the temptation to correct him," Rachel replied lightly. But underneath her smile, she was still mulling over why FBI agents were coming aboard the ship and whether there was a money issue that Easter Balch had uncovered. *Could she have been working for the FBI rather than the NYPD?*

Chapter 14

Rachel's parents had been keen to explore
the Puerto Rican rainforest as soon as
they had seen the itinerary. Rachel was
just as enthusiastic about it, but she was
concerned the terrain might be too harsh
for Marjorie. Rachel's elderly friend
brooked no argument over the matter,
insisting she was fit enough to walk the
mile or so that would be required.

"Are you sure about this, Marjorie?"
Rachel asked again as they waited for a
taxi to take them to the departure location.

"Absolutely. It's described as an easy
activity level outing, and as long as I take
it slowly and use my trusty walking stick,
I'll be fine. Don't worry, Rachel; if I can't

manage, I'll perch on a rock somewhere and wait for you to come back for me. I can't miss the opportunity – I've always wanted to visit a rainforest, you know."

Rachel nodded as they got into the taxi. At the departure point, they would meet with other guests from the ship before taking a guided excursion through parts of the rainforest. Rachel was sorry that Sarah wouldn't be joining them, partly because of her friend's love of nature, but also because she would know what to do if Marjorie had an accident. When they arrived at their destination, Rachel was delighted to see Brigitte and Gwen were taking the tour. She beamed at the two nurses.

"I know what you're thinking, you know," scolded Marjorie.

Rachel put her arm around her. "You can never be too safe."

"Mm, perhaps you're right."

Rachel's father was already brimming with excitement and the tour hadn't even started. Other taxis were pulling up all the time, dropping off passengers. A tour guide told them they would be led in groups of ten at a time, and as they were already in a group of six, they just needed four more to join them.

"What about you four ladies?" asked the guide. Rachel turned to see who he was speaking to and noticed there were four young women, standing chatting to one side. The male tour guide's eyes lit up at the sight of them; he'd already tried to flirt with Rachel until Brigitte had told him to get on with his job in her usual assertive-cum-brusque manner. On this occasion, Rachel had been happy for the French nurse's directness.

Now as she looked at the four women who had joined them, she couldn't help thinking she had seen them before, but where?

Marjorie rolled her eyes. "Now we'll be lucky if we learn anything, as I do think that young man's attention will be elsewhere."

"Not for long," said Susan. An older man was directing the smarmy young guide towards a middle-aged group, simultaneously bringing a female guide over towards their own gathering.

"This is Carla," he said. "She will be taking you on a wonderful tour of the El Yunque Rainforest today. Please stay close at all times and be careful. Although the paths are well trodden, it has been particularly dry this year and there can be surface dust, which becomes slippery." He looked at Marjorie, but chose not to say anything further when Rachel took her arm protectively.

"That's good to know, thank you," said Rachel. "We'll be careful, and we have two of the ship's nurses for company."

The man appeared satisfied with this. "As you wish. You have all signed disclaimers, I take it?"

"We have indeed," answered Gwen, "so you can be sure you won't be sued, unless there's any negligence on your part."

The man was about to respond, but was grabbed by another guide wanting him to delegate her to a group.

Carla smiled at them and, with an American accent, welcomed them to the tour. She explained that she had learned English in New York, having lived there for ten years before returning to her home country after university.

"You won't believe it," she said laughing, "but I was a nun for a while."

Rachel's eyes met Marjorie's as the elderly lady's eyebrows rose. Her parents were too fascinated by the surrounding flora already on display to be paying much attention. Brendan had been happy when Rachel had called him first thing to let him know she wouldn't be joining a nunnery, albeit temporarily, and he was even more pleased he wouldn't be forced to lie to his wife. With all of that behind him, Brendan was now in a hurry to get started on one of the highlights of his holiday.

Carla lifted a blue tour sign with the number 1 painted in the centre.

"Oh goody. We're not only the first, but we're the blue group!" Marjorie said gleefully.

"Trust you," Rachel laughed. "As long as we don't see a blue light on the way round—"

Brendan's grin demonstrated the joke was not lost on him either. Rachel felt a flutter of excitement herself, having never been anywhere like this before.

"This is going to be amazing," she said, forgetting all her earlier worries about Marjorie.

The tour guide started walking with Rachel's parents immediately behind, followed by the four women who Rachel still couldn't place. Rachel, Marjorie, Gwen and Brigitte were at the rear. Marjorie started well, but soon slowed as the guide trudged on at pace through the forest. Rachel slowed her own pace to match Marjorie's.

"Do you want us to stay with you?" asked Gwen.

"No, you go on ahead, but tell the guide to slow down a little. It looks like they've stopped up there anyway," Rachel replied.

"I'm sorry," said Marjorie. "Perhaps I shouldn't have come. I don't want to ruin your day out."

"You're not ruining it. The guide is going too fast, you were walking at a steady pace. Mum won't let them leave us behind, even if Dad gets distracted."

"It is rather beautiful, I wouldn't blame him."

Rachel smiled. Within a few minutes they had caught up with the main group that had stopped to examine fauna.

"Where do we know those young women from?" Marjorie asked.

"You too? I don't know, perhaps they are part of the entertainment team or crew."

Rachel heard the guide pointing out tree orchids to their right and noticed two of the young women engaged in conversation with her father. They were laughing together over something. The guide came to join Rachel and Marjorie.

"There are lots of stops along the way, so don't worry about the pace. You will always catch up and we won't go on without you."

"That's good to know," said Rachel.

"You could also slow down a little," said Brigitte, "so that we can all appreciate the surroundings at leisure. I don't think we are in a race, are we?"

"I'll see what I can do, but you have to remember there is another group behind us, and groups behind them – we leave at fifteen minute intervals to allow for stragglers, but we can only wait so long."

Rachel was pleased Marjorie was engaged in conversation with Susan and Gwen about the colours of the orchids, otherwise she would have been embarrassed.

"Nevertheless, you're going a bit too fast even for me." A white lie wouldn't hurt.

Carla nodded. "Of course."

After ten minutes of milling around admiring the scenery and the flowers, they set off again and Carla was true to her word, meandering rather than power walking. Marjorie had no trouble keeping up, apart from on the inclines, where she slowed down to catch her breath.

The morning passed in pleasant harmony. The temperatures were a little cooler, but more humid inside the forest, the tree canopies providing welcome shade from the hot sun. Every so often they stopped to listen to the sounds of birdlife or if Carla saw something she thought they would enjoy. Finally, they arrived at a beautiful waterfall they had heard from a distance.

"This is La Coca Falls, a popular attraction for our visitors," explained Carla. "Those of you who wish to can climb to the top via those rocks." She pointed. "I'll come too."

Rachel looked at Marjorie.

"You go, dear. I'll be fine here, I'm enjoying the view."

"I'm staying too," said Brigitte. "I don't like climbing."

The rest of the party headed up the rocks. The waterfall was not that big, so Rachel reached the top in no time. When her father joined her, they waved to Brigitte and Marjorie.

"Is Marjorie all right?" he asked.

"Yes, she's fine now the pace is more leisurely. I'm pleased she came, she's like a child in a toy shop."

"Me too, Rachel. I do love ecology, as you know, and this is such a treat for us. Come along, Susan."

Rachel heard voices as the other women arrived at the top, walking out of sight with Carla to explore further while Gwen and Susan joined Rachel and her father.

"I didn't realise those four were nuns," Gwen said.

"That's where I've seen them before. Is that why you were so friendly with them, Dad?"

"Yes, they recognised me from the service the other day. Nice girls."

"I'm baffled. They seem such a strict order, and yet here they are in mufti," Susan remarked.

"Ah, well it's because they are noviciates. They are given a little more leeway than the ones who have gone through the vow process. Also, they are a relaxed order when in the city, apparently. Some of the women who have taken their vows wear normal clothes when visiting friends and family."

The conversation was brought to an end as the young women returned alongside Carla, who seemed overly friendly with them. Everything about these women piqued Rachel's interest and her instincts screamed that all was not as it seemed.

"Cheryl, wait for me." She heard the familiar voice of Angeline calling out to the freckle-faced woman who was racing down the rocks.

"That's where I recognise the South American accent from," Rachel muttered to Gwen. "They are in our art class, Marjorie and I have been chatting to them over the past two days."

"Strange they didn't say hello."

"I was thinking the same thing. We didn't recognise them out of their habits, so perhaps they thought we were the ones being ignorant. I think I'll have a little catch up when we get back down."

Gwen chuckled. "Yeah, of course you will. They do look different, don't they?"

When Susan was out of earshot, Brendan whispered, "Rachel, I thought the chief had told you to steer clear. I would rather you heeded his advice. This place is far too pleasant to be spoiled by your natural curiosity."

"Come on, Dad, I just want to say hello and ask a few innocent questions. Maybe they'll be more open out of uniform."

Her father sighed, nodding. "Be careful. Although I think these women seem harmless enough – I can't imagine any of them being dangerous."

"Of course not." Rachel started the downward scramble before her father had time to say anything else.

"It's the nuns from our art class," she whispered to Marjorie when she joined her at the bottom of the falls. Marjorie wagged a finger in recognition as the four young nuns joined the two of them.

"Hi, Cheryl. Sorry we didn't recognise you out of your habits."

"No problem." The Canadian woman smiled, shaking Marjorie's hand. "Good to see you again. Angeline, it's our friends from the art class."

"Hello." Angeline nodded, but didn't shake hands. She was generally more standoffish, verging on sulky.

"It's a small world, isn't it?" said Rachel.

"Mm. Look, here's Letitia and Blethyn." Cheryl seemed happy to talk.

"Charmed to meet you all again. I feel exceptionally safe now we have all areas covered," said Marjorie.

"What do you mean?" snapped Angeline.

"Medical and spiritual – we have it all. Those two are nurses from the *Coral Queen*." Marjorie nodded in the direction of Gwen and Brigitte.

"Oh, I see what you mean." Letitia was the only one to produce a broad smile, revealing bright white teeth. Without the habit, Rachel could see she had beautiful copper red hair that flowed down her back and her aquamarine eyes shone with mirth.

"I love your accent; where is it from? I can't remember whether we asked before," said Rachel.

"I am originally from Uzbekistan. We are an international order with noviciates from the four corners of the globe."

Rachel nudged Marjorie as the twinkle in her friend's eye told her she was about to point out that a globe is round.

"Time to move on," called Carla, glaring at Letitia and Cheryl. Angeline and Blethyn, who hadn't spoken, immediately joined the guide, while Cheryl and Letitia followed behind with Rachel and Marjorie. Rachel's parents created a gap between the two groups, with Brigitte and Gwen straggling at the back. The atmosphere in Rachel's group lightened without the dour Blethyn to bring them down.

"It must be fascinating to be a nun. Did I tell you I always wanted to join an order?" Rachel caught herself saying, much to the amusement of Marjorie, although her only giveaway was an upturned lip and a raised eyebrow.

"Really? Me too," said Letitia. "I went to a convent school, and although I rebelled for a while, I felt called to serve. I wasn't drawn to conventional convents, but there was something different about the Order of the Blue Light – that's the order we belong to – and I couldn't wait to follow my calling. Mother Cross tells me I was born to be a nun."

"That must feel good to know you're in the right place. I have so many doubts. What is it about your order that is different?" asked Rachel casually.

"I'm not sure really. The leadership is charismatic and exciting. Mother Cross tells us we are called to make a real difference in the world. Sister Murdoch draws a lot of women in, but I'm a Mother Cross fan."

"The order does sound interesting. I'd love to hear more about the leadership and what your order teaches. As you know, my father's a vicar."

"No offence," said Cheryl, "but we're called to be separated from the world, unlike your father. Although your parents seem nice."

Rachel squeezed Marjorie's arm to prevent her coming up with some retort in defence of her parents.

"I can see how that could be attractive, but how can you make a difference to the world if you are separate from it?" she asked with furrowed brow.

"We are going to cleanse the world one area at a time," said Cheryl.

"How?" asked Marjorie.

"I'm not sure. We haven't been told that yet, but that's why we are on this cruise: to make a difference."

"Those that don't follow are doomed," said Letitia. "That's what Sister Murdoch tells us anyway. She does most of the teaching. The other nuns are a bit more old-fashioned."

"Sister Sage, Sister Backus!" Blethyn called the two women away. "Look at this."

Cheryl shrugged. "Sorry, got to go. They don't like us talking too much and they're in charge when the elders aren't here, hence the formal tone."

"Stuff and nonsense," said Marjorie as soon as the girls were out of earshot.

"I agree, worrying talk, that," said Gwen. "I was listening from back here. Sounds like brainwashing to me."

"That sort of talk scares me," said Brigitte. "What is a noviciate anyway?"

"It's a term used to describe someone training to become a nun, and for other religious training such as being ordained," explained Rachel. "It comes from the word novice."

"Ah, now I understand. I'm all for religion, but what do they mean?" Brigitte continued.

"I don't know," said Rachel, "but I'm determined to find out, because it sounds like they have imminent plans to change our bit of the world."

"You mean people on board the *Coral*?" asked Marjorie.

"I'm not sure, but whatever this order is up to, it is secretive and comes more from Sister Murdoch than anyone else, by the sounds of it. Why wouldn't they know what the plans are if they are innocent? The '*are* doomed' bit sounded like she means it will happen soon, that's what scares me."

"Good point about the secrecy," said Gwen.

"Secrecy is power," said Marjorie. "It could just be the bait that keeps them following. Many secret organisations drip-feed information to the lower ranks – look at the Masons."

As they caught up with the group that had stopped at its next point of interest, Blethyn appeared to be giving Cheryl and

Letitia a scolding. Marjorie could be right. There was obviously a pecking order within the noviciates, and Blethyn liked it rather too much.

Rachel got out her phone to take photos of their surroundings, making sure she took pictures of each nun's face and added their names to the saved files. Marjorie nudged her as Carla turned her way and she did a 360 with the phone as if taking a video.

"Smile, Mum," she called while Marjorie distracted Carla with a question.

"This seems to be some sort of meeting," whispered Marjorie later. "That Carla appears to know Angeline and Blethyn."

"I'm thinking the same thing," said Rachel. "It seemed odd our guide was changed at the last minute, and Carla behaves like a person with something to hide. I wish I knew what it was and what they're up to. Clandestine meetings are never a good thing."

"If you ask me, they've all got something to hide. That's part of the attraction for vulnerable women, isn't it? They're running away from something. All will be revealed in due course. We'll just have to work out what it is."

Chapter 15

The taxi pulled up at the dockside and dropped Marjorie, Rachel and her parents off where Sarah was waiting.

"Did you have a good day?"

"Enlightening," said Rachel.

"Most interesting," said Brendan. "We loved the rainforest. The habitat is perfect for the ecosystem. I could have spent days out there looking at the orchids alone."

"I know what you mean. I've been four times and would have happily joined you again today, but I needed the sleep. It was a busy night."

"So we heard. We bumped into Waverley this morning." Rachel rolled her eyes.

"We met Brigitte and Gwen on the same trip," Marjorie chipped in. "They took a taxi into the centre of San Juan."

After a few minutes, the older Princes excused themselves to go for a walk.

"I think I'll go back on board now and leave you two young things to go off by yourselves for a while," said Marjorie.

"You don't have to," said Sarah.

"I know, but I am a little tired after our excursion. I do need to take it easy at my age, you know. Remember our meeting at six o'clock, Rachel."

Rachel nodded. "Glad you reminded me, I'd forgotten. Are you still all right to eat ashore afterwards?"

"Oh yes, I'll be fine after a few hours' rest. I'll be dressed and ready before His Lordship arrives."

The ship wouldn't be sailing again until 10pm, which gave them a rare opportunity to taste the local cuisine in the evening. They had arranged to eat with Rachel's parents, Sarah and Jason, who had both managed to get the evening off.

"What's that six o'clock thing all about?"

"Marjorie's summoned Waverley to her room for a meeting later. Well, not quite summoned – he suggested it, but she tied him down to time and place."

Sarah frowned. "I knew the two of you wouldn't keep your noses out of that woman's death. Waverley has enough on his mind. What did you mean when you said enlightening? I'm assuming you weren't referring to the rainforest."

Rachel filled Sarah in on the day's activities and their encounter with the four nuns.

"Apart from the bit about people who don't follow being doomed sounding a fraction sinister, it could be normal evangelical talk with regards to the order's ability to gain converts. They certainly seem to attract young people, so there must be something charismatic about it."

"There's charisma all right, but I'm not sure it's innocent. I think it's one of those sects that attracts emotionally vulnerable women. Letitia is a sweet girl, but an ardent follower. The one that looks like a witch, Sister Murdoch, appears to have woven a spell over quite a few of the women. I think where she leads, most of them will follow. Her influence is greater than that of Mother Cross, except where Angeline and Letitia are concerned. Angeline was jealous of the attention shown to Easter Balch by the Mother Superior. Cheryl and Letitia seem genuinely caught up with loyalty to the whole order, but they're not familiar with the teachings. That in itself is odd, although Marjorie says it could be like the Masons: the further up the chain you are, the more knowledge you gain. I didn't like Blethyn before today, but even less so now. The whole thing screams sect to me. I just hope it's not one of those suicidal ones."

"But surely if they hold to Catholic teachings, life is sacrosanct?"

"Good point. I'd still like to check out what their teachings are and learn more about their plans. Remember, Sarah, a woman has died, possibly as a result of infiltrating this group or because of something she discovered. That doesn't make it wholesome, now does it?"

"That's true if she was murdered by someone within the order, and if she was murdered at all. Doubt's been cast upon that now. Not that Graham or Waverley are happy about it."

"What do you mean?"

226

"We were having tea earlier when Waverley barged into Gwen's office with one of his angry faces on. I thought he was going to burst a blood vessel he was so annoyed. His face had that red glow to it, you know the one?"

"All too well. Don't tell me, it was something to do with the FBI."

"Yep. Apparently they are now convinced that Easter Balch died of an accidental overdose of digitalis, or even suicide."

"Do they have any reason for thinking either of those two things are likely? Dr Bentley told Gloria Franks suicide was unlikely as there was no note."

"They say there is evidence that many of the women in the order come from unstable backgrounds. Easter had apparently dabbled with drugs in the past."

"I'm not surprised about the backgrounds bit, although Blethyn and Letitia's families sound stable. The drugs part could fit with Easter's mum telling us she got in with the wrong people after her father died – or was it while he was drinking? I suppose her father being an alcoholic didn't help."

"She had been a heavy drinker herself at some point, according to the post mortem, but that wasn't responsible for her death. The FBI agents have concluded that everything points to a digitalis overdose resulting in a convulsion and a heart attack, and whether it was accident or suicide, they don't believe there is a motive for anyone to have killed her."

"I don't believe it. What about the mention of Armageddon and the fact the woman worked for the NYPD?"

"They say your father could be mistaken about what he heard, or that the nun may have been hallucinating as she died, and they still won't say whether she worked for the NYPD. Graham did concede that delirium could have occurred with a digitalis overdose. The FBI have recommended closing the case with regards to a suspicious death. They have concluded that Easter was a probable ex-junkie who couldn't live up to the rules within a religious order. The senior nuns have confirmed she was rebellious and prone to temper tantrums."

"This all sounds a little too convenient to me. Maybe she was delirious and hallucinating following an overdose, but I still think she had uncovered something that got her killed. Whether it's to do with the apocalypse or not, she was murdered, of that I'm certain. I overheard a conversation in the chapel this morning that makes me think that's the case. I was hoping to speak to Waverley about it – I'd almost forgotten about it myself until now. It's been such a lovely day out, I got lost in my surroundings. This is a beautiful island."

"What did you hear?"

Rachel recounted the conversation she had overheard between Cheryl and Angeline, the presence of Cooper and his suspicious behaviour, and the mysterious involvement of Colin Bell.

"So, you see, that and the conversation Marjorie and I had with Cheryl and Letitia in the rainforest point to something strange at best and malicious at worst. We just need to find out which. Where do the FBI agents say she got the digitalis from, and how could it have been an accidental overdose?"

"Ah, well that is a bit of a mystery, but Waverley did discover that another one of the older nuns, Sister Faith Martin, takes digoxin for an irregular heart beat."

"Where do they get these names from?"
Rachel giggled.

"Mother Cross admitted Sister Faith –
that's what they call her – is forever
leaving tablets lying around. There are
yellow, brown, red and white ones, and
the coroner explained the brown ones
could have been mistaken for senna, a
laxative."

Rachel thought for a moment. "So
they're suggesting it's possible that an
intelligent young woman who may or
may not have worked for the NYPD
mistakenly took a heart tablet instead of a
laxative. I can't believe I'm hearing this."

"I feared this reaction, Rachel. Whilst it
wouldn't be the most common mistake to
make, it is plausible, yes. You just won't
let it drop, will you? What if it is just a set
of innocent, albeit tragic, coincidences
and you're wrong for once in your life?"

Sarah's voice had risen more than usual, and Rachel quietened her own tone.

"Then I'll be happy to admit it, but too many coincidences amount to conspiracy and criminality in my world."

Sarah put her arm through her friend's. "Well, just this once, Rachel Prince, I'm counting on you being put in your place when it all turns out to be nothing. A woman died, I was there. It looked very much like a convulsion to me and her symptoms in retrospect fit with the theory of digitalis overdose. The women around her seemed genuinely shocked. Whether it was a deliberate or accidental overdose resulting in a heart attack is, I admit, as yet unknown. But you know as well as I do that if she had struggled with addiction in the past, it could lead to either type of overdose."

"If she was an ex-addict, I'll concede on that point, but none of the other nuns have alluded to that type of past, and I think, in view of the fact she wasn't popular, it would have come out. They would have been the first to mention it."

"Unless she and Mother Cross kept it to themselves. You said they were close."

Rachel thought for a moment. What Sarah said could make sense.

"That's another thing. Why were they close? She was relatively new to the order, from what I gather. I still think it's a suspicious death. Remember, this order seems to pride itself on choosing beautiful young women who don't appear to have any blemishes – other than the odd freckle. They wouldn't take someone with drug problems, if you get the pun."

"What if she didn't tell them? I'm sure they don't do background checks on new recruits."

"Good try, Watson, but this is murder in my book. Do you want to know why?"

"Not really, but you're going to tell me anyway."

"Because my gut tells me so."

Both women laughed hysterically. Rachel's gut was not to be ignored, as previous investigations had shown.

Chapter 16

Rachel's parents, Sarah and Jason agreed to walk to the restaurant in the Old City, but Rachel suggested she and Marjorie would take a taxi and order wine ready for their arrival.

"You could have walked, you know. I would have been fine taking a taxi by myself," Marjorie complained.

Rachel looked at her fondly. "I don't doubt it, but I'm tired after our ramble through the rainforest. Anyway, I wanted to talk to you about why Waverley cancelled and my conversation with Sarah."

"It's perhaps as well he did cancel, because your parents wanted to leave earlier than planned. Now I realise why."

"They do love walking. At home they walk for miles in the countryside whenever they get the chance. Although that's not often, as they are busier than ever now."

"It's the way of the world these days. One day, people will realise that they have rushed around for years and their lives will almost be over and they will not be able to remember what all the hurry was about."

"That's deep, Marjorie."

"Ignore me. It's just an old woman's ruminations, that's all. Now, you were going to tell me why His Lordship cancelled."

Rachel repeated the conversation she'd had with Sarah earlier and what had happened while they were off ship.

"I never did have much time for the FBI. That poor woman deserves better. I thought there was some other reason they were involved, too. Looks like we're arriving. Perhaps we'll discuss what we are going to do about it later."

Rachel squeezed Marjorie's arm as the taxi dropped them off outside the renowned José Enrique building, which looked more like someone's veranda than a well-known eating hotspot. The area was bustling with tourists; a lot of passengers from the cruise ship were clearly taking advantage of a rare non-sailing evening.

Rachel discovered that she needed to put her name and phone number on a board just inside the gates.

"How long is the wait?" she asked one of the staff.

"You're lucky this evening; it's only about half-hour, miss. Some people decided they didn't want to wait, so we've sent them on to other local places."

"Thank you." Rachel looked at Marjorie. "That will give the others time to get here. Shall we sit over the road?"

Marjorie nodded. They found a bar where they could sit watching the crowds arriving at the restaurant from every direction and following the same procedure as they had just done. The bright pink exterior stood out, even though it seemed there was a competition for the brightest coloured building in the area.

"I think we got here just in time," remarked Rachel.

"I read in the *Coral News* this place is good, but I didn't expect it to be quite so busy. It's run by an up-and-coming chef, I believe."

"Good job we came by taxi, or I'm not sure we would have had time to eat and get back to the ship."

Rachel's phone rang just as her parents and friends came along the street. She answered, waving for them to hurry. A few minutes later, they were all seated.

Rachel was excited at the prospect of tasting some genuine Puerto Rican cuisine. The dining area was as busy inside as it had been out, with menus displayed on large whiteboards propped up around the room.

"Sorry, we didn't get the opportunity to order any drinks. In fact, we're lucky to have got a table in such a short space of time, according to a man we spoke to over the road."

"We should have known," said Sarah. "Almost every time I've been to San Juan, I've worked in the evening. Once I went to the Marmalade Restaurant, but that's more American. This uses locally sourced ingredients, which is why I suggested it. Lots of the Puerto Rican crew come here for lunch and dinner when we are in port, so it comes highly recommended."

"Well, we did get a table, so I suggest we order before it's too late to return to the ship." Brendan nodded towards a waiter whom he'd managed to make eye contact with. "Not that I would mind another day here. We could return to the rainforest."

Rachel hoped her father wasn't regretting joining a cruise rather than taking a more traditional holiday, but she consoled herself with the fact that her mother was enjoying the luxury of life aboard ship.

There followed an evening of gastronomic delights, with each of them experimenting by eating something they had never tried before. Rachel enjoyed watching Sarah challenge herself to try something new. It was harder for Sarah and Jason to choose, as the ship's chefs provided themed restaurant evenings and could conjure up just about anything from any country in the world. The *Coral* stocked up on local foods at each port, her freezers containing enough meat for each cruise and some extra for unforeseen circumstances or delays.

"You could try the catch of the day. It's listed over there," suggested Jason. It was filleted tiger grouper served with rice and beans.

Sarah grinned and nodded to the waiter.

"I'll have the same," Jason decided. Rachel and Marjorie almost opted for mahimahi because Marjorie liked the name, but then discovered it was dolphin and neither of them could bring themselves to order it. Instead they settled for mofongo, a speciality of Puerto Rico. Rachel's parents ordered pollo, a local chicken dish sautéed in butter and served with a paella-type rice and beans.

The restaurant was not overrated and did not disappoint. For a moment, Rachel forgot all about nuns, conspiracy and her annoyance with the FBI as she enjoyed spending time in the company of her best friends and family. The only thing missing was Carlos. She hoped he was all right as the funeral had taken place today. With the time difference, she worked out it had probably been happening while she, her parents and Marjorie were waiting for their taxi this morning.

"Are you all right, Rachel?" asked her mother.

"Yes, sorry. I was just thinking about Carlos. It's the funeral today."

"Who was it who died? I haven't had the chance to ask." Sarah looked apologetic.

"An aunt. They were close when he was younger, as she lived with them in London until his parents returned to Italy. She used to take him to play football in the park while his sister went to extra art classes. She's an interior designer now – his sister, that is. She used to do his paperwork before moving to Derby."

"I know a little of his family, because he tells me about them when he comes to visit," said Marjorie.

Rachel raised an eyebrow. Carlos was occasionally employed to look into matters involving the business Marjorie owned. Although her son, Jeremy, now ran the business, Marjorie liked to maintain an interest. There had been a few attempts at takeovers and theft, so Carlos was sometimes called in to investigate when Jeremy felt it was outside the scope of their own internal security. Marjorie and Carlos got on well and he would sometimes call her if he was passing her way after being on a case. He also met with her at home to discuss any findings during the investigations he undertook for Jeremy. Jeremy had been abrupt in the beginning, but once Carlos and Rachel had got to know him, they formed a mutual acceptance, although Rachel still found Marjorie's son a hard man to like.

"I think we had better get a move on." Jason's voice broke through her musings.

The party took two separate taxis back to the ship and Rachel's parents decided it was time to call it a night. After checking that Marjorie wasn't too worn-out, and being reassured to the contrary, the rest of them agreed to go for a drink in the Jazz

Bar. Rachel wanted an update from Jason on the FBI.

Chapter 17

"We need to talk about Easter Balch," Rachel said as soon as they were sitting with drinks in front of them.

"There's nothing to talk about. The case is closed," said Jason, frowning.

"Like heck it is," said Marjorie. "That group is up to something, Jason, and if we don't find out what, someone will get away with murder."

Jason took a gulp of lemonade. "Like what? The coroner's concluded digitalis overdose, the feds dismissed foul play, and they told Waverley they are standing the NYPD down. They don't think there's anything going on."

"Jason, don't tell me you're falling for that?" said Rachel, exasperated.

"I would thank you two to leave Jason alone," said Sarah defensively. "He's doing his job, and anyway it's none of your business, Rachel Prince. Nor – with respect – yours, Marjorie."

"Those nuns were up to something in San Juan today," retorted Marjorie. "We believe at least two of them were known to the tour guide and held a clandestine meeting, and – with equal respect, Sarah – you weren't there."

The last thing Rachel wanted at this moment was a falling out between friends. They were all tired, she and Marjorie had had a long day, Sarah had been up most of the night, and Jason was most likely protecting his boss. It was time to dial down the tension.

"Okay, perhaps it was a tragic case of accidental overdose. Anyway, Marjorie,

I'm tired. Shall we leave these two lovebirds alone?"

Marjorie took the hint. "Yes, quite right. Apologies, you two, it's been a long day. We'll catch up tomorrow, Sarah."

Rachel said goodnight and led Marjorie away by the arm before she was tempted to mention Armageddon or Brimstone Hill. The ship would be docking in St Kitts the following day.

"You're not tired at all, I can see your cogs churning," Marjorie said as they headed towards the lifts.

"No, but obviously Jason's under orders to toe the line, whether he wants to or not. I don't think he believes it's natural causes at all, he wasn't that convincing."

"What makes you think that? He sounded pretty certain to me."

"He couldn't look at me while he was talking. That's not Jason at all. He's always good with eye contact. He hasn't let it go, and neither has Waverley from what Sarah said earlier about how upset he was after meeting the FBI. Whatever Sarah's saying now, she's trying to protect us and her fiancé. Unless Jason hasn't been completely honest with her, which is not likely."

"I see, so it's back to two investigations and ne'er the twain shall meet," laughed Marjorie.

"Oh, they'll meet eventually, once we have to go to the chief with anything we find. We do need to be careful, though, Marjorie. I think someone in this group is dangerous – maybe more than one – and we don't know how many we are dealing with. I suspect it will be more than one and could involve the majority, we just don't know yet. Easter may have taken someone into her confidence, or she may have been in the wrong place and found out something that got her killed. I don't believe she accidentally overdosed and I'm certainly not falling for suicide."

"Do you think Cheryl told someone else that she overheard an odd telephone call?"

"Not sure. I don't think she knows of any dubious plans. She sounded seriously worried when I overheard her telling Angeline about the call."

"What about Angeline?"

"We'll put a question mark in front of her. I was thinking she was innocent until I watched her with Blethyn today. Then there's Letitia, who said those who don't follow are doomed."

"She could just have been referring to hell. That's not a new Christian teaching."

"If that were the case, I wouldn't be concerned. Heaven and hell are basic fundamentals of Christian belief and concerned with the afterlife. It's whether it relates to those in this life that worries me – that reference to Armageddon still gives me the creeps."

"Well, let's hope it's the former. They could just be one of those groups that believe Armageddon is going to occur any minute. Perhaps they believe something supernatural might happen tomorrow at Brimstone Hill. They wouldn't be the first cult to set a date and find they were wrong."

"I do hope you're right, Marjorie. The other thing is that Dr Bentley agreed that a digitalis overdose could bring on a hallucination, so the Armageddon thing might be a red herring."

"I do hope they haven't suggested the girl took her own life to Gloria. The poor woman's been through enough."

"Hopefully they were out for the day and evening like we were."

"Anyway, it *has* been a long day. Why don't we call it a night? We'll watch them closely tomorrow while we are out. It's perhaps as well your father also booked the outing to Brimstone, isn't it?"

"Yes, it is. I do wish I could talk to Waverley about this and ask him about background checks on these women. He told Mother Cross about his original plan for me to infiltrate the order, so we need to know who she is and whether we can trust her. She could be a formidable ally."

"Or enemy," replied Marjorie.

"Or enemy," repeated Rachel.

Marjorie couldn't sleep. Visions of danger occupied her mind. Her greatest concern was that if the Mother Superior was involved in any dirty dealings, then her young friend was in danger.

Surely His Lordship would be aware of that. But sometimes the man can be a complete idiot. She tossed and turned, exasperated with the security chief. If anything happened to Rachel, she would never forgive him.

Finally she gave up on sleep and switched on the overhead light. The ship was sailing through the night – should she call for room service? She decided against it and looked at her bedside clock: 1am. It hadn't been all that long since she had got into bed.

Heaving a huge sigh, Marjorie pulled on the blue dress she kept for casual wear. She thought it would be good to belong to the trouser brigade at this moment, but it was not in her DNA to wear such things.

"Snellthorpe, you're too set in your ways," she mumbled out loud.

Marjorie opened the balcony doors and stared up at the star-studded sky behind the ship for a while. It was beautiful. Lights from cargo vessels could be seen in the distance, but otherwise all was dark across the water. Tonight the beauty was in the sky, although the lapping of the waves against the stern added impact.

Cramp in her right calf was annoying and uncomfortable; it was one of the many things that came with age. She sighed again. She did have more aches and pains these days, and truth be told, the walk through the rainforest had taken it out of her, but she wouldn't have missed it at any price. Well aware that time was no longer on her side, she took advantage of every opportunity to experience something new and was willing to pay the physical price for it afterwards. If it were just the physical, she could deal with it, but the thoughts whirring around in her head tonight were dark and foreboding.

A young woman, maybe a policewoman, taken in her prime. Her fear for Rachel grew.

Then there are these silly girls chasing after religion for all the wrong reasons, believing they can escape from the world and whatever it is they're hiding from. Letitia and Cheryl seemed to be nice young women, but one was obsessed with the Mother Superior while the other was a nervous wreck, from what Marjorie could see.

What are they doing with a convent that tells them beauty is a sin? They were either naive, vulnerable or hiding something.

The other two, Angeline and Blethyn, Marjorie hadn't taken to – a bit too holier than thou for her. That alone she could deal with, but they seemed to have a nasty streak, all too competitive. Rachel and her parents had a faith that Marjorie could only aspire to, but they remained in tune with others and tried to do good in the world.

That's what religion should be about, not hiding yourself away from people and renouncing things that don't matter. Beauty is a gift, surely?

Marjorie didn't like where her thoughts were taking her, so she decided to get out. Shaking her head, as if by doing so she'd make the marauding notions vanish, she left the suite and made her way downstairs to the atrium. After mulling over the death of Easter Balch and the multiple scenarios that might have led to it in her head, she decided to visit one of the all-night bars.

The Piano Lounge was lit up with groups of people still enjoying drinks and company. Marjorie found a quiet table – there were quite a few free tables, as it happened – and ordered a brandy from the waitress, who appeared within seconds of her being seated.

"Late night, ma'am?"

"Couldn't sleep," Marjorie replied, looking up at the tired woman smiling down at her.

The woman nodded understanding and disappeared to the bar at the far end to get the drink. Marjorie followed her path before taking a look around the room. It was occupied by mainly middle-aged or elderly people; younger people would probably be in the discos or the livelier bars.

The waitress returned with her drink.

"Are you on all night?" Marjorie asked.

"Yes, ma'am, until we close at 5am. Are you enjoying your cruise?"

"Immensely, thank you. We had a lovely trip to the rainforest today – an amazing place. Have you been?"

"Yes, my husband and I went once."

"It must be wonderful travelling the world. Do you like working for Queen Cruises?"

"I do. I've worked for a few cruise lines, but Queen is one of the best, and as you say, I get to see the world. When we get time off, that is."

Marjorie understood this, aware that the crew's time ashore was limited, but it was still a good and generally safe way to travel the world.

"I'm almost envious. I take it you're American, Charlene?" Marjorie picked up the name from the waitress's badge.

"Yes, can't lose the accent. I'm from South Carolina. My husband works on board too, in the restaurant. You may have met him – Colin Bell."

Marjorie's ears pricked up. "Ah, our maître d?"

"Of course, most people know him."

"I expect he's fast asleep, isn't he? I know he works long days."

"You would usually be right, but not tonight. For some reason, he's over there with some guests."

Marjorie followed the direction of Charlene's nod and saw Colin huddled together with the obnoxious Cooper. Sister Murdoch was just visible from behind a pillar – Marjorie recognised her from the extra weight she carried and the crooked nose. Blethyn was also there.

"Well, he's in good company, I see."

Charlene raised her eyebrows. "I don't get it. No offence if you're religious, but it's not the sort of company he normally keeps. I think they must be friends of Abe's."

"Abe?"

"Yes, the man they're sitting with. Colin knows him from his college days. They were friends for years, then something happened. After that, they hardly spoke, and now they're, as you see—"

"Friends again," finished Marjorie.

"Charlie?" a middle-aged man at a table nearby called. The waitress rolled her eyes.

"Some people insist on calling me Charlie when my name's Charlene. As you noticed, it says Charlene on my badge." She shrugged. "Still, duty calls. I'd better go, enjoy your drink."

"Thank you, I will."

Marjorie's eyes were firmly fixed on the company across the room. Her only wish was that she had sat a little closer so that she could hear what they were saying. It was too late to move now, though. Charlene would wonder what she was doing and she knew better than to make it obvious she was staring.

Whatever they were speaking about seemed to be important and secretive. Marjorie couldn't help thinking how out of place the two nuns – Blethyn was now back in her habit – looked in what was in effect a lounge bar. Perhaps the order was more progressive than she had initially thought. Someone might have mentioned it today, but her memory played tricks sometimes.

It was a shame that the pleasant Colin Bell could be mixed up in something untoward, although he might not be involved in anything at all. His wife had said Abraham – Abe – Cooper and he had known each other since their schooldays, so it could be an innocent meeting of old friends. Abe – she must remember to tell Rachel Cooper's first name, as it might be important. Perhaps Sister Murdoch had been at the same college? She was about the right age. People weren't born nuns; it was something they chose to do later.

After draining her brandy glass, Marjorie decided it was no good staying any longer. She couldn't hear what was being said and her eyes were beginning to feel heavy; she could nod off in the bar if she wasn't careful. That wouldn't look good at all.

On her way back to her room, Marjorie had the feeling she was being watched – a feeling that sent shivers through her spine. The last time she had felt this way, it had been true. She looked around and thought she could make out a shadow further down the corridor, but whoever it was turned towards one of the rooms. While they did so, she decided to pick up the pace, proud it was still possible for her to hurry when necessary, and made her way along the corridor. At the next stairwell and lift entrance, she took a left turn and summoned a lift. Marjorie pressed the button for deck sixteen before reversing out of the lift and crossing over into the next corridor, where she stood panting with her back to the wall.

Heavy feet hurried towards the lift, and then she heard a gruff huffing sound and footsteps taking the stairs up to the next floor. Marjorie could feel her chest pounding and, looking down, she realised that her hands were trembling. Bracing herself, she took a deep breath and followed the corridor to the end before turning right to cross back to the portside again. Almost falling into her room, Marjorie sat on the bed, shaking, for a good ten minutes before her heart finally slowed down, visions of the cruise where she had first met Rachel – and been pursued by a merciless killer – flashing through her troubled mind.

Chapter 18

Waverley sat at his desk shuffling papers. "I'm not surprised Rachel Prince is pushing us to continue investigating, Goodridge, but we've got nothing to go on. According to the FBI it was death by misadventure or suicide. I can't really see the woman overdosing herself, but it could have been an accident. The mistaken pill theory could have caused the death like they suggest."

"What about the word she uttered to Mr Prince, sir? He's convinced there was no mix-up with what he heard. He doesn't strike me as melodramatic, either. I don't like the fact no-one will tell us whether Easter Balch worked for the NYPD.

Surely if she didn't, they would just say so. And if she was a nun, there could be a warped killer on board. Sorry, sir, I don't buy the suicide or accident theories."

"The thought of a nun-killer has been giving me sleepless nights. Having said that, she was an ex-addict, according to the FBI, and didn't her mother tell the Princes she had got involved with the wrong people? I don't buy the fact that there is some mysterious apocalyptic plan being set in motion, either. Sometimes it's the simplest explanation that's the right one."

"Sir, I've fought against extremists and they are capable of anything. ISIS don't have the monopoly on martyrdom or a willingness to kill those they believe are infidels. History and past wars tell us this. What if that is what we're dealing with here? Easter Balch found out what was going on and was silenced. Her last word was Armageddon, not 'Tell my mum I love her' or 'Help me' or anything like that. Armageddon. What if that woman gave her life to warn us of an impending catastrophe? Don't we owe it to her – and everyone else – to carry on investigating?"

"I would have agreed with you on that supposition until Graham Bentley confirmed that a digitalis overdose could result in hallucinations, Goodridge. No, I really don't think that's the issue here. No doubt we'll both be pleased once the visit to Brimstone Hill Fortress is over and done with. Mother Cross seems to be a sensible woman, not some extremist. Nothing she has said to me suggests she is in charge of an order of fruitcakes, and she's as sane as I am.

"What she did say, that backs up the accidental overdose theory, is that Sister Faith, one of the older nuns, takes regular digoxin and is always leaving her pills lying around the place. She also admitted that the sister could be forgetful – take that to mean demented. She's an ex-nurse, apparently, and sometimes tries to give the other nuns tablets. They know to humour the old girl, but not take the pills. Mother Cross thinks she told Easter Balch about it as she was new to the order, but she can't be certain. If she did forget to warn the girl, the theory about mistaking them for senna tablets rings true. Perhaps it was just a tragic accident."

Waverley was now reacting as Jason had expected him to: listening but not taking his concerns seriously enough. Jason held one last card.

"Rachel has never been wrong before, and she says there's something strange going on. Lady Snellthorpe is convinced too. They both maintain they picked up on suspicious behaviour among the nuns ashore today, sir."

"What suspicious behaviour?" Waverley coughed, the stress clearly getting to him.

"I didn't give them the chance to say, sir. I, erm, cut them off and told them they should not be involved."

"Why?"

Because I was obeying your orders was what Jason wanted to say, but instead he chose his words carefully.

"I was trying to dissuade them from meddling, sir, and getting into trouble."

"Yes, quite right, Goodridge. They saw something, though – you're certain of that?"

"It would seem so, sir. They went to the rainforest and four of the nuns were on the same walking tour as them, that's all I know. I think Rachel has other stuff to tell us, but we haven't talked to her."

"Why is it that girl is always around when there's trouble? And why am I starting to believe you? Okay, I don't go along with the Armageddon thing, or with lethal nuns roaming around the ship, but I suppose there could be someone out to make it look that way. Rachel mentioned a man called Cooper, who seemed to know Colin Bell. Perhaps that's the place to start. Track Colin down and find out if there's anything amiss."

"Do you want me to interview him, sir?"

"No, just observe for now. I don't want to upset a trusted employee, and if he is involved in something, I don't want to tip him off either. We need to do this on the quiet; I don't want Captain Jenson finding out. He's given me direct orders to drop it. I'll pull up Cooper's records in the morning, assuming there's only one

Cooper travelling. They didn't get a first name?"

"No, sir. He's with a wife, though. Rachel noticed a wedding ring."

"Good, that makes it easier. I'll also give this Detective Rodrigues from the NYPD a call, see if he can tell us anything more about what his detective – if she was one – was working on. Either that or he needs to give me a firm denial. You're right about one thing, Goodridge: we owe it to the dead woman to investigate a little further, just to be sure."

Jason left the chief's office with a bounce in his step. He trusted Rachel's instincts, and Graham Bentley thought an accidental overdose unlikely. He didn't rule out suicide, but didn't rate it as likely, either. Jason's biggest concern was the dying woman's last word to Rachel's father.

His fear was one he hadn't voiced to anyone, and hardly dared admit to himself. He hoped the FBI was not covering up anything that put the passengers and crew of this ship in danger. His mind was in overdrive – what if they were hiding the effects of some new toxin? Flashbacks to the effects of chemical warfare still gave him nightmares, even when he was awake. Many of his colleagues had turned to drink over the issue, but he had witnessed too many drink-fuelled arguments between his parents as a young boy to go that way. Nevertheless, the thought of some sort of nerve weapon was too horrendous to contemplate, but it had to be something major to bring out the FBI.

It was vital the security team find out what was happening. He agreed with his boss that a group of nuns were unlikely terrorists and that Easter Balch's death could have been caused by a tragic mistake. But at the back of his mind, the question remained; he needed to talk to someone about his fears, because at times they were overwhelming.

Jason kept his distance from Colin Bell as he shadowed the man. The Coral Restaurant had closed for the evening and Jason watched as the maître d met with various head waiters from the galley. They ate in the staff restaurant, and Jason debated with himself whether he should just go to bed. Sleep deprivation worsened his flashbacks.

He hadn't slept since the nun had been killed, and today had been a long day as he'd had to cover for Waverley while he'd been with the agents from the FBI. There had been an issue with a crewman who had been extorting money from crew members. They could ill afford to pay it back, so one of them had reported the man. On top of that, a passenger had been found to have a large quantity of cocaine in his suitcase. The room steward had entered the man's stateroom by mistake while he was in the shower. Thankfully she had kept her wits about her and left the room without being noticed, calling security straight away. Jason had been able to apprehend the man, who had been travelling under a false passport, and hand him in to the port authorities in Puerto Rico. He had then arranged to have cameras and microphones installed into the reported crewman's room. The next time he did any blackmailing, he would be caught.

Jason was brought back to the present as he saw Colin check his watch and leave the restaurant. It was around midnight and Jason thought he would be heading to bed, but instead the maître d entered the Piano Lounge and took a seat at a table in a corner. Feeling in his pocket, Jason realised he still had a spare listening bug from setting up surveillance in the crewman's room earlier. He took the opportunity to plant it while Colin went to the bar to speak to his wife, casually passing the table and slipping his hand underneath, placing the device on the underside before walking to the far end of the bar, well out of sight.

Jason often used the Piano Bar to catch up on paperwork because he liked the atmosphere and the music was generally quieter than in some of the other bars. He also liked the speciality coffee.

"Good evening, Officer. The usual?"

A small, round waiter stood beside his table. Jason was relieved it wasn't Charlene, Bell's wife.

"Yes please, Ronnie, extra strong. I've got a lot of paperwork to catch up on."

Jason took the laptop out of his bag and fired it up. The coffee arrived, and once he was satisfied he was not going to be seen, he discreetly inserted the earpiece into his left ear.

He heard a man join Colin Bell and risked a quick peek. From the description Rachel had given, he surmised it was Cooper. They needed to look into this man and find out what he was up to. Rachel had mentioned Cooper had been with a woman she'd assumed was his wife, but there was no woman with him tonight.

Jason struggled with interference and feedback vibrating through the earpiece and couldn't make out what the two men were talking about. As he heard more people arrive, he stretched right to take another quick look.

Nuns! Now this is interesting.

He fiddled with the settings on the laptop and changed channel for the listening device on his earpiece. The sound was clearer, but the volume was low.

This is dismal. I must have a word with the boss about this equipment.

After twiddling buttons for a few minutes and connecting a portable booster, he was finally able to hear parts of the conversation.

"Plans are in place. There's no stopping us now." The voice sounded like that of an older woman.

"Are you sure this will work?" Bell's voice.

"Of course it will," snapped Cooper.

"Shush!" The younger woman spoke. "Look there. She keeps turning up wherever we are. She was on our tour today."

Jason's heart sank as he watched Lady Snellthorpe enter the bar and take a seat on the opposite side of the room. She hadn't noticed the huddled group. Their voices lowered to whispers and he had to fiddle with the volume again to listen in. It was hopeless; he was too far away to get any sort of decent signal, and there was outside interference that was getting louder. Frustrated, he put the equipment away and downed the coffee in one.

He watched Lady Snellthorpe chatting to Charlene, and then Charlene pointed over to her husband. Lady Snellthorpe's body language altered – a dead giveaway to anyone watching her, although he couldn't see whether the group was taking any further interest in her.

After Lady Snellthorpe finished her drink, she left the bar. Jason got up and saw the younger nun leave at the same time. This didn't look good, so Jason decided to follow to check if it was a coincidence. Lady Snellthorpe got into a lift, and the nun got into the one next to it. By the time Jason reached the lifts, both had stopped at deck fifteen. He raced up the ten flights of stairs – not easy on a cruise ship as they were spiral, but he was as fit as ever and arrived just a couple of minutes behind the lifts.

He popped his head around the corner to see into the corridor, panting slightly. The nun had disappeared, but there was a man standing outside a stateroom door in the corridor, looking as if he was going in. Lady Snellthorpe had stopped walking, but then she started up again, moving faster along the corridor. The man followed.

Jason was pleased to see Lady Snellthorpe turn left at the next lift stop. He waited to see if the man did the same, and when he did, Jason hurried along the corridor in time to see him running up the stairs. Jason paused, hearing Lady Snellthorpe's heavy breathing.

Wily old thing! She had clearly realised she was being followed, pressed the button and sent an empty lift to the next floor. He heard Lady Snellthorpe moving again and followed her until he saw she'd returned safely to her room.

But why? Was someone on to her and Rachel? How could that be?

Jason returned to his own room and called Waverley, letting him know about the meeting between Colin Bell, the man he assumed was Cooper and two of the nuns.

"So you didn't get to hear the conversation in any detail?"

"Not really, sir, just something about a plan being in place, but that could mean anything. There was something else, though."

Waverley's sigh told Jason that his boss realised he wasn't going to like what he was about to say next.

"Lady Snellthorpe came into the bar, and she was followed when she left."

"What? Who the heck by?" Waverley asked.

Jason explained about the nun leaving at the same time, heading up to deck fifteen, and then the man in the corridor. He couldn't resist laughing when he recounted the subterfuge Lady Snellthorpe had used.

"What was she doing there in the first place?" snapped Waverley.

"I don't know, sir. It could have been an innocent case of insomnia."

"There's no such thing as innocence between her and Rachel Prince. They need to watch they don't become the hunted, Goodridge. I don't see why anyone would follow Lady Snellthorpe, though, unless she's been indiscreet."

"I agree, sir."

"What did she say about it?"

"I didn't speak to her, sir. I didn't want to alarm her."

"Did you identify the man following her?"

"I didn't. I was keeping my distance. Six foot, broad build, wearing a black dinner suit."

"Like thousands of other passengers on this ship. That's just great, Goodridge. Someone else to add to the mix. I can't believe it."

"He might not have been following, sir. It could be coincidence. People do get the wrong rooms, as you know. I've had at least two calls this cruise from frightened women, alarmed by drunks on the wrong floor."

"That's true. It does seem unlikely that anyone would want to follow a harmless old woman, I suppose."

Jason wasn't sure he'd describe Lady Snellthorpe as a harmless old woman; she had a sharp brain and a quick wit. If she was being followed, she had managed to lose the tail like a pro.

"It does, sir, really. And the nun could have been returning to her room, although I didn't capture any sign of her. Do we know what deck the religious order is on?"

"Let me just check." Jason heard a few strikes of the keyboard. "Afraid they're on deck seven and mostly in interior rooms – fits with the vow of poverty and simplicity. She could have been going to the upper decks for a stroll outside."

"Maybe. Anyway, as I say, she was nowhere to be seen when I made it up to deck fifteen. Are you still in the office, sir?"

"Yes, just checking a few things. Get some sleep, Goodridge. You're taking an impromptu day off tomorrow and joining the Prince party on a trip to Brimstone Hill Fortress while I do background checks. I want that group watched closely, so I need you to be on full alert."

Chapter 19

Rachel joined Marjorie for breakfast and was alarmed to hear about the previous night's events. She frowned.

"You should have called me."

"And said what? I had a feeling I was being followed? Now, in the light of day, I think it could have been some innocent man trying to find his room after a few too many drinks." Marjorie was being dismissive, but the slight flicker of her eyebrow was something Rachel had noticed occurred when her friend was stressed. She would chat to Waverley about this later and see if there was any CCTV footage.

"We were right about the links between Colin Bell, Cooper and the nuns, though. Well done, Marjorie. Any more insomnia, though, and you either stay in your room or I'm coming with you."

"Oh, don't fuss."

Rachel's second frown in as many minutes achieved the desired result. Marjorie conceded.

"All right, terms agreed. Now what are we going to do about this new information?"

"Nothing at the moment, because we need to get going. We're meeting my parents and Sarah in the main atrium in half an hour."

"So we are. I'd better get dressed." Marjorie finished her tea. Rachel marvelled at how her friend could make drinking tea look so elegant.

"What?"

"Nothing. You're amazing, that's all." Rachel kissed her on the cheek and hurried back to her room to get ready for the day.

Thirty minutes later, they were in the main atrium with Rachel's parents and Sarah. Sarah's face lit up as a casually dressed Jason arrived wearing Bermuda shorts and a pink vest. She beamed at him.

"I thought you were working today?"

"The boss gave me the day off. Is it all right for me to tag along?"

"You're most welcome," answered Brendan.

Rachel sidled up to the happy couple. "The boss gave you a day off, did he?"

Jason smirked. "He can be kind, you know. I've been working hard; perhaps he thought I needed a break."

"Yep, and I'm a brass monkey. You don't fool me for one second, Jason Goodridge."

"What do you mean?" asked Sarah. Turning to Jason, she then thumped him playfully on the chest. "You're working!"

He grinned and kissed her forehead.

"Well, I'm still pleased to have you along in any capacity," she said, cheeks blushing with pleasure.

"Shall we go? The tour bus is over there," Susan suggested.

"Oh, I am looking forward to today," said Marjorie.

"Really?" teased Jason. "You're looking a bit peaky to me – anyone would think you'd been up half the night."

Rachel turned to say something, but Jason bounced ahead of them. He was clearly happy to be out with them for the day, even if he was on duty.

"Did you bump into Jason last night?" she asked Marjorie.

"No, I would have told you. Perhaps someone told him. Word gets around on this ship, doesn't it?"

"Mm," replied Rachel, not convinced. If Jason had seen Marjorie last night, who else had, and was she now in danger? Rachel took her arm protectively, determined nothing would happen to her friend. She'd rather stop investigating than put Marjorie in danger, but the nagging feeling that it might be too late for that was disconcerting.

Rachel was not surprised to find the nuns already walking around the grassed area of the car park when they arrived at the part of Brimstone Hill where cars could go no further. The gaggle of blue habits blended into the horizon and they almost moved as one. It was a beautifully sunny day, and the warmth and bright sky made her feel that nothing could go wrong with her world. Even her father had donned khaki knee-length shorts as the sun would be hot out in the open. Her mum looked stunning in a brightly printed cotton dress.

"I can see where you get your looks from," said Marjorie, loud enough for Susan to hear the compliment and flash a smile in their direction. Rachel wore a white cotton dress that Carlos had bought her for the holiday. It made her feel like he was with her, and the thought brought the familiar warmth.

"You're glowing, Rachel," said Sarah, walking towards her.

Rachel sighed. "I was just thinking of Carlos. And you can talk!"

They had decided to hire a six-seater taxi to take them up to Brimstone Hill Fortress, as it would have been too steep for Marjorie to climb from the entrance further down the road. Once they arrived at the car park, Sarah, Marjorie and Rachel linked arms and followed the tour guide on the flat, taking in their surroundings. Brendan was interested in the military history and so, it seemed, was Jason. Rachel had studied history at university, so she too was listening intently to the local guide.

The fortress could only be accessed by a steep climb, but they could see the walls from where they were, and cannons were strategically placed on the cliff edge all around where the taxi would wait for them. The walls of the fortress were remarkably well-preserved, as far as Rachel could see, which was hardly surprising – Brimstone Hill Fortress was listed as a UNESCO World Heritage site.

"I'm afraid it does have a rather chequered history," said Brendan. "It was designed by us Brits, but built by African slave labour."

"Part of our colonial history, then," said Marjorie.

"Yes, but it did keep the island safe."

"Who from?"

"The French," Brendan answered. "The French and the British fought over all the West Indian islands. This island's named after St Christopher, of course, and shortened to St Kitts."

Rachel noticed that Jason was listening to her father, but had one eye on the holy order that was drifting left. She was also constantly distracted by the group of nuns. Cheryl waved when she caught her looking. Rachel waved back as if she were just out on a tour – which, in fact, she was.

Rachel scanned the nuns to see where Sister Murdoch and Blethyn were, having heard about their clandestine meeting with the obnoxious Cooper and Colin Bell. She couldn't see either of them, but it was a large party and some of the nuns had turned a bend. Rachel couldn't help wondering what Colin Bell's involvement with this group was – she'd had him down as a traditional family man.

"What are you thinking about? As if I need to ask," said Jason, who had appeared at her right shoulder.

"As you say, you don't need to ask. What was that flippant remark about earlier? Did you see Marjorie last night?"

"I did. I was carrying out surveillance on our maître d."

"Ah, Colin Bell. That explains it."

"Tell me you didn't put her up to it."

"You can't possibly believe I would have done that! I would never put Marjorie in danger. I only found out about it this morning. It was a genuine serendipitous encounter. She couldn't

292

sleep, so she went to the Piano Lounge for a drink to help her settle. She got talking to Colin's wife, and then she noticed who Colin was with. I assume you know?"

"I do."

"Jason, she thinks she may have been followed afterwards. Did you notice anything?"

"Come on, you two, you're dawdling."

"Right behind you, Mum."

"I did," whispered Jason. "We'll meet up later and talk about it. I'm not sure if someone is on to her; the young nun recognised her when she entered the bar."

"That was Blethyn. Marjorie told me she and Sister Murdoch met with Colin and that horrible man, Cooper. This puts a different slant on things. I think Blethyn's involved up to her eyes in whatever this is all about. It wouldn't surprise me if Angeline's in with them, too."

Rachel's parents joined them.

"It's time for the climb. Your father wants to learn more about the history of the place."

Rachel suggested that Marjorie take a stroll around the flat part of the site.

"Looking at that climb, dear. On this occasion, I will concede."

"I'll walk with Marjorie around here," Sarah offered. "I've been up there once before. You two go ahead, I know you've got things on your mind."

"What things?" asked Susan.

"Jason wants to take photos for his family," Rachel improvised.

"Race you," said Jason, smirking.

"You're on," replied Rachel, taking off at a sprint.

The nuns had already started up the slope before Rachel and Jason, who arrived at the top, breathless and panting.

"You won," Rachel gasped. The slope had been steeper than it looked, and although she was an excellent runner, the hills she negotiated at home were nothing like this.

"Army training," said Jason, smiling. "And now I use the running machine on the highest incline setting before passengers are awake."

Jason nodded in the direction of the nuns, who were moving away from the main fortress towards a ruin. This gave Rachel and Jason the opportunity to stay close to the nuns without being seen. They ambled after the party, making sure they left enough space between themselves and the nuns.

The group had now assembled into the large company that it was. Rachel and Jason leaned over a cannon, looking through a turret to where the nuns were congregated.

"So, did you hear anything last night?" Rachel asked once she'd managed to bring her breathing down to normal.

"Not really; I think there was something wrong with the signal. I just couldn't get a clear sound, even when I switched frequency."

"And how much surveillance equipment do you have in place at the present time, Officer Goodridge?"

"That would be telling, DS Prince. None of it needs concern your inquisitive nature, though, so forget it."

They paused when the group ahead of them started moving again.

"I think we need to get closer," said Rachel.

"Aye, let's split up. I'll flank the right and you go left. Stay out of sight."

"That shouldn't be hard, they seem to be praying. I'll try to get within earshot if possible." Rachel crouched down and, keeping close to the ruined walls, headed to the left. There were a few trees, more cannon, small dark rooms that led nowhere and some archways providing enough shelter initially, but the final part was more open. While hiding behind a rock doorway for a few minutes, she decided to take her chance, as the nuns were still absorbed in prayer. Crawling along the cobbled paving covered with moss and grass, which seemed longer than it had appeared, she managed to get within ten yards of the group.

They were out of the way of the majority of tourists who had wandered around to the main fortress, so she settled behind yet another large cannon, hoping her father wouldn't stick his head through the turret affording a view of where she was. With that risk in mind, she pretended to inspect the side of the cannon while peeping through the gaps.

Someone was speaking, but the voice was lost to her at first. Dialling in, she recognised Mother Cross leading the rest of the nuns in prayer. Rachel's surveillance was made easier by the fact that all the heads were bowed where the nuns stood around a cross – something that had been added recently, she thought, as it didn't look old at all. There was a lot of genuflection and signing of the cross going on.

In the distance, Jason was on the other side of the large courtyard, closer to where the Mother Superior stood, so she decided to move towards the next cannon where she could get closer to the nun fuelling her interest, Sister Murdoch. The older nun was standing on the left fringe of the gathering, easily identifiable due to her dark-grey habit contrasting with the blue mass. The other four grey habited nuns were on Jason's side. Rachel hid behind the cannon and heard Mother Cross's voice echoing back from the ruined wall behind.

Jason was no longer in her line of sight, but her interest was piqued by Sister Murdoch and Angeline whispering. The two women were ignoring the rally call to pray for the lost as Mother Cross's voice rose by several decibels. Rachel was surprised as Angeline had seemed devoted to the Mother Superior – perhaps she had switched allegiance. The rally call was followed by prolonged and passionate chanting and repentance.

Another two nuns joined Sister Murdoch, who was now swiftly passing something to each one of her companions. Rachel couldn't see clearly what it was, or who the other two nuns were, but she guessed one would be Blethyn. She craned her neck to get a closer look.

The rest of the nuns stopped chanting up on the hill, and an eerie silence followed. Rachel froze. She tried to control her breathing as she felt her own heart beating. It was against her character to be spying on nuns, but one among their company had died in suspicious circumstances.

She'd decided to take another chance at getting a better look at Sister Murdoch when suddenly, a hand smothered her mouth and she was tugged back behind the large cannon. Trying to struggle, she found it was hopeless. The arms that held her were too strong.

"Don't struggle and I'll let go."

Rachel nodded and her assailant did as he'd promised. She turned around and her mouth dropped open.

"What the heck?"

Chapter 20

Colin Bell held a finger to his lips as they sat behind the cannon. He pointed to a doorway; she nodded and followed. They entered a small, dark storage room and waited for the nuns to return to the main fortress before stepping back out into the courtyard. The sun beat down on her face and she felt a pounding in the back of her head as she tried to assess whether she was in any danger.

"I owe you an explanation, Miss Prince."

"You certainly do. What are you doing here and why did you sneak up on me like that?"

"I saw you and Jason Goodridge heading over here after the nuns came this way. I could see you from that turret." He nodded to the one Rachel had noticed earlier. "I just wanted to check you weren't in any danger."

"And why would you think that?"

"I'm not sure really, but I believe something is going on with that lot."

"By that lot, I assume you mean the nuns. Any idea what?" Rachel wasn't about to trust the maître d just yet; he might be fishing for information to see how much she knew.

"No, I'm sorry, I don't, but there are some shady dealings and I think a friend could be involved."

"Abraham Cooper?"

"Ah, so you have picked up on him, then. I thought you might have done."

"I only know he's an ignorant moron and he may have met with one or two of the nuns – not to mention you, Mr Bell."

His face flushed. "Look, Miss Prince, Abe was a good friend at college, but we parted ways when he got involved with a crowd that weren't afraid to push the boundaries of the law. It wasn't my thing. I tried to warn him, he wouldn't listen, end of story. We followed different paths and haven't spoken in years."

"You may as well call me Rachel as you nearly suffocated me," she laughed.

"In that case, please call me Colin."

"Okay, Colin. So how did you hook up again?"

"Quite by accident. He's now an events manager, can you believe, for a billionaire who sponsors holy orders like this one, arranging regular holidays for multiple congregations around the world. Says he earns good money from it too. I'm in charge of sorting out a private bash after we leave St Thomas on Day Seven. We've been meeting up to finalise arrangements."

The previous night's meeting between Cooper, the two nuns and Colin now made sense. Colin appeared to be telling the truth, but she wasn't quite convinced yet.

"So why do you think there's something shady – as you call it – going on?"

"The death of a nun, for one thing: secret conversations, Abe's behaviour, and that nun, Mora Murdoch. There's evil in those eyes."

Rachel noted the first name of Sister Murdoch for future reference. "Do you think the nun's death was suspicious?"

"I don't know; I'm just a humble maître d, but there was no real chatter within the congregation after her death. The waiters listen out for such things. Gossip brightens up their lives."

"I must remember that next time I'm dining. So you're suggesting that with a sudden death, there would usually be some discussion over meals?"

"Precisely, that's when people let their guard down. Waiters, like taxi drivers, are invisible. This lot didn't even mention it. I tried to bring it up over a drink when we were planning the do – offered my condolences – but Mora Murdoch shut me down instantly. Snapped my head off, to be frank."

"Okay, but here's a question. Do you think your friend Abe is capable of murder?"

"When I knew him, no. He was small-time, but ambitious. Now he's swanky, wears expensive jewellery and goes around like he owns the world. He always had the potential to be like that, loved undermining people. He was a bully, really; another reason we went our separate ways. I didn't like the way he treated people back then, but it only came back to me when I noticed how he behaved at dinner. I've had to pull him up during the cruise for being rude to other passengers before anyone complains. He's arrogant, thinks he can get away with it, but you and I know he could be escorted off ship if his behaviour turns violent. He even slapped a passenger yesterday, but didn't realise I saw it. I'd rather not be involved with him at all, if I'm honest, but I'm in charge of their private party, so I have no choice."

"Do you know who's invited to this private do?"

"All I know is it's for one hundred and nine guests, including the nuns."

"Do you have a guest list?"

"Not yet; that's another big secret. The invitations will be going out the day before, when we're in Antigua. I did hear Abe bragging to that woman he's with over dinner that this cruise was going to make him a fortune."

"She's not his wife, then?"

"He passes her off as his wife, but I'm not certain she is. They don't behave like a married couple to me. More like a business relationship, if you ask me."

At that moment, their conversation was cut short as Jason arrived. His brow shot up, but Rachel shook her head.

"I'll leave you now, Miss Prince, erm, Rachel. Perhaps we will talk again."

"Oh, I'm sure of it, Colin."

"What was that all about?" asked Jason.

"He grabbed me from behind – I thought I was a goner for a minute, but I don't think he's up to anything. Says he was worried about me. I'll tell you all about it later; I can see Mum and Dad over there. Shall we go back up?"

After rejoining Rachel's parents, they made their way down the incline to the flat area where they had left Marjorie and Sarah. Jason ran over to his fiancée, who was staring out over the cliff towards the sea. Marjorie was sitting on a rock. By the time Rachel joined them, Jason had explained what had happened up at the fortress.

"Rachel, I wish you would stay out of danger. You could have been killed. What if it had been someone else?" said Sarah.

Rachel rubbed her eyebrow thoughtfully. "I don't think they suspect I'm anything but a tourist just yet, and if they wanted me dead, I've no doubt I would be."

"That might be the case, dear, but perhaps we should back away while we

still can. That's two near misses now."
Marjorie's voice sounded a little shaky.

"What do you mean, two near misses?"
asked Sarah, eyes widening. Marjorie
explained briefly about the night before
and how she'd felt she may have been
followed after leaving the Piano Lounge.

"Right, that's enough. Marjorie,
Rachel, do you hear? Enough." Sarah's
voice had risen by several decibels.

Before Rachel had the opportunity to
reply, her parents joined them.

"Is everything all right? Rachel, what's
the matter?"

"I'm fine, Mum. Too much sun, that's
all. That run didn't help; it made me feel a
bit queasy. Jason has given me lots of
water and now I feel better."

A concerned looking Brendan Prince
looked on. "Is that it?" he asked Jason.
Rachel pleaded with her eyes, so Jason
nodded.

"Yes, sir."

"Well, let's get back into town," said Susan. "There are some nice-looking cafés I noticed on the drive up here. You'll feel better with some food inside you. I do wish you young people would wear hats."

Rachel resisted the temptation of pointing out that her mother wasn't wearing a hat either.

"Yes, Mum, so you've said before."

"Your father and I had a lovely time up there. It was so interesting, he'll fill you in once we get back to town. I'm feeling a bit warm myself now."

Rachel was desperate to compare notes with Jason and share more of her conversation with Colin Bell, so her thoughts were far away from military history. Had Colin's intentions been malicious, she could have easily been killed. She had let her guard down and almost paid the ultimate price. Her demeanour was poised, she knew, so no-one would realise that inwardly she was shaking; she had learned to control adrenaline surges and their subsequent effects on the body. Pushing her hands into her shorts pockets, she stilled any tremors that could be picked up by her eagle-eyed mother. At least there had been no Armageddon up at Brimstone Hill Fortress.

Perhaps that's being kept until the private party.

Chapter 21

There hadn't been much time to change
for dinner when they got back to the ship,
and Rachel's parents were keen for her
and Marjorie to join them for the evening
show afterwards, so it was 10pm by the
time the two of them met up with Sarah in
the Jazz Bar for a tête-à-tête. Marjorie
was beside herself with excitement,
Rachel could tell as they found a booth
and ordered drinks.

Drinks had just arrived when Jason
appeared.

"You're late," said Sarah.

"Sorry. I've also got some bad news: I
have to go and help Ravanos separate
some warring families, and then we've all

been summoned to Waverley's office. See you there in a bit, unless there's trouble."

"Oh dear, that doesn't sound good," said Marjorie, her excitement waning.

"What, the family factions or the Waverley thing?" Rachel joked.

"Both, actually, but more the latter."

"Do you know why we've been summoned, Sarah?" Rachel wondered if her best friend had told Waverley about her encounter with Colin Bell, but on reflection thought Jason would be more likely to have informed his boss. She wanted a chat with Waverley anyway, so this would be a good opportunity.

"No. I collected the on-call bag from Bernard, then went straight to evening surgery when we got back. I haven't even spoken to the rest of the team; I dashed up here straight afterwards. Here's Bernard, perhaps he knows something."

"Good evening, ladies." The cheery smile lifted the mood around the table as the male nurse joined them. "Beer please, Christa," he called over to one of the passing barmaids. "Did you have a good day ashore? More importantly, have you solved our 'non-case' yet?"

Sarah punched him playfully on the arm. "Have you heard any news tonight? Jason's just summoned us all to Waverley's office."

"Sorry, I can't say I have. I had a busy day dealing with more passengers with sunburn. As soon as you took the on-call bag from me, I went to bed. I was up most of last night. Day off tomorrow; I'm heading to the beach. I expect you're going to be told to stay off the non-murder case – as if that would work!"

"That could be it," said Rachel. "Perhaps the FBI has been on to Waverley again. He told Jason he was going to contact the NYPD detective. I expect he's had a telling off, and now he wants to pass that on to us."

"I can't say I'll be sorry if you are told to back off – not that you'll listen," said Sarah.

Rachel sympathised with her friend, who saw enough trauma in her job as a nurse without worrying about Rachel and Marjorie's safety. She finished her martini and lemonade.

"Let's go and find out, shall we? The suspense is killing me."

Waverley's office on deck three was in darkness when they arrived, so they found seats nearby while they waited. They sat quietly; Rachel hadn't yet told Sarah and Marjorie about her conversation with Colin Bell, but she thought she might as well tell everyone at once when they were all together with Waverley and Jason.

Jason arrived first. "Sorry, it took a bit longer than expected."

"What was it all about?" asked Marjorie.

"Two families vying for sun loungers, would you believe? It seems they have been falling out every day since they came on board and it came to a head today. They've been at it all day, according to the pool staff. Part of the argument is over one family's daughter being told to stay away from the other family's son." He smirked.

Sarah rolled her eyes and shook her head. "As if you haven't got enough to do. How did you solve it?"

"I told them if security was called to deal with them again, one person from each family would be put under house arrest for the rest of the cruise."

Sarah laughed. "I can see how that would have solved the problem."

"I felt like banging their heads together."

"Banging whose heads together?" Waverley appeared behind Jason.

"The McIlroys and the Browns."

"Oh them. They're the least of our worries. Come on through."

The quartet followed Waverley as he opened up his office. He motioned them to take seats around the table, where there was a two-seater sofa and two armchairs. Jason perched on the arm of the chair where Sarah sat, leaving a chair free for his boss.

"I need a drink. Would anyone like to join me?"

"I won't say no to a Scotch, Chief," said Marjorie.

"Water for me, I'm on call," said Sarah.

"Tonic water, Goodridge?"

"Yes, sir."

"Same for me," added Rachel.

Waverley got on the phone and requested the drinks. He did keep a supply in his office, but on this occasion he chose to call down to hospitality. He flopped down in the vacant chair and sighed heavily before coughing, a sure warning something bad would follow.

"Have you told them anything?" He looked at Jason.

"No, sir, no time."

"Well, don't keep us waiting any longer. What is it and why are we here?" said Marjorie.

Waverley coughed again. "As you are aware, I was told yesterday that the death of Easter Balch was no longer being treated as suspicious. Goodridge and I discussed this last night and we weren't totally convinced. I asked him to tail Colin Bell, who appears to have some links to the man you found suspicious, Rachel."

"I have news on the Colin front," she said.

"Yes, we'd all like to know about that," said Sarah.

The chief appeared annoyed at the interruption. "Quite. We'll come to that shortly. Anyway, Goodridge followed Bell to the Piano Lounge, where he met with Abraham Cooper, Sister Mora Murdoch and Sister Blethyn Lee. He tried to listen in using our latest wireless bugging device – we managed to purchase a supply before our tax year was due to end. I have to say, the equipment is state of the art – we've had considerable success."

Marjorie tutted impatiently. "And did Jason manage to hear anything with this wonderful new addition to your armoury?"

"Not really," said Jason. "There was a lot of interference. I just picked up a few words about a plan being in place. I also heard them being shushed when you came into the bar, Lady Snellthorpe."

"Marjorie," she corrected.

"Yes, Marjorie. Blethyn Lee told them she recognised you from their tour that day and other encounters, then cautioned them to be quieter. Blethyn left soon after you did, in fact."

"I did feel I was being followed. I thought I saw a man in the corridor, though, not a nun."

"You did."

Marjorie looked up at Jason.

"Sorry, Lady… erm, Marjorie. I followed the sister, but by the time I'd run up ten flights of stairs, she had disappeared. I did see a man in the corridor who may have been following you. I checked you were okay and admired the way you lost him."

"Thank you. Although it was alarming. Do you think I was being followed?"

"Can't say for certain; it could have been a case of wrong room, and I didn't get a clear look at him."

"However," interrupted Waverley, "we have gone through the CCTV footage today and can't find any evidence that Sister Lee followed you at all. The puzzling thing is we can't find any footage of her again until this morning. I expect she got off on a lower deck. Sometimes our CCTV jams and we lose bits."

"Did you notice her get off earlier, Jason?" asked Marjorie.

"Sorry, no. I was too busy running up to deck fifteen."

"How convenient for her that it stuck at exactly the same time she followed Marjorie," said Rachel. "Are there any time gaps?"

"Not that we can find," answered Waverley.

"So who got out of the lift on Marjorie's floor?" asked Sarah.

"The man who appeared to have been following – or not. I'm inclined to believe not, Marjorie," answered Waverley.

Rachel gasped. "Hang on. Did you track down this man?"

Waverley coughed again. "I'm afraid not; he was lost in a crowd and we didn't have a clear enough image to differentiate his face from others with our cameras. We have over three thousand guests on board, and until we get facial recognition software, which is highly unlikely bearing in mind how expensive it is, we can't always identify people without sending images to the authorities. Such requests have to be supported by evidence."

"Not to mention the facial recognition controversy," said Rachel.

"Exactly. I'm inclined to think it was an innocent case of mistaken room after too much alcohol."

Marjorie snorted. Waverley looked sheepishly towards the elderly woman. Rachel patted her arm reassuringly.

"If you were followed, Marjorie, we will find him," Waverley said. "Now, moving on. Today I called Detective Rodrigues of the NYPD. I can tell you that he's not at all happy that the case of Easter Balch has been dropped so readily by the FBI. I had to drag information out of him, but he finally admitted that, although she wasn't employed by the NYPD, she was working on his behalf."

"So she wasn't a nun after all," said Rachel, exhaling in relief.

"Actually, she was a nun, but she also happened to be the detective's niece."

A group gasp filled the room.

"He had a tip-off that there might be some deal going down on board the *Coral Queen* and that it had something to do with a religious order. When he discovered his niece had joined the order recently, he took it as divine intervention and thought he'd hit the jackpot."

"Until it all went terribly wrong and his niece was murdered." Marjorie spoke quietly.

"I can only imagine how he feels about that," said Waverley. "The man's only venting anger at present, but I suspect he's feeling as much guilt as rage. He'd told her that if the nun thing didn't work out, he'd find a job for her in his department. Felt she had the potential to be a rising star."

"What about the drug history?" asked Rachel, already knowing the answer.

"Fiction. She's never been in trouble, apart from a warning from a landlord when her friends had a fight in her accommodation. There had been some heavy drinking – hardly surprising as her father was an alcoholic and died as a result of the stuff – but no drugs. He doesn't believe his niece had ever taken drugs."

"That is interesting," said Rachel. "Any hints of why the FBI would say she had?"

"No. In fact, he clammed up immediately afterwards, as if realising he'd said too much. I think he's a man who speaks first and thinks later."

"In that case, you're probably related," muttered Marjorie, just loud enough for Rachel to hear and grin. Waverley carried on, having not heard.

"There is something else I need to tell you all. Something which has convinced me to rigorously investigate the death of Easter Balch again – not that I wasn't going to continue after speaking to Rodrigues today."

They were interrupted by the arrival of the drinks. Once the waiter had left, Waverley threw back his whisky in one gulp.

"What is it, man?" snapped Marjorie.

"A passenger went missing while on shore today. We put out multiple alerts before we set sail, but they didn't turn up. You may have heard the announcements."

"No, I went straight for a shower." Rachel gulped back some tonic water, concerned about what might be coming next.

"I heard the announcements requesting a passenger contact reception, but didn't catch a name," Marjorie added.

"We thought the passenger had missed the ship. This sort of thing happens from time to time, and we can't wait very long. We did wait longer than usual because of who it was, but when there was no response, we left."

"Sarah's told me that you've left people behind in the past, and we are warned every day in the *Coral News* to be aboard on time. Who are you talking about?" asked Rachel. "I assume there is a connection to Easter."

"You're right, Rachel. There is a connection. I'm afraid a body was found out near Brimstone Hill Fortress. The dead woman has been identified as Mrs Gloria Franks."

Waverley rubbed his imaginary hair back from his forehead. Rachel's mouth dropped open. Marjorie knocked back her Scotch.

"What did she die of?" asked Rachel.

"Suspected overdose."

"Again! The mother of Easter Balch dies in the same way as her daughter."

Waverley nodded. "Connor Franks told us his wife had been devastated by the death of her daughter. He believes she went to the fortress in place of Easter to honour the pilgrimage and that she must have found it all too much. She was found pretty close to the pilgrimage site."

"I bet he does – convenient that mother and daughter die. I expect he can now lay his hands on the poor woman's fortune," said Marjorie, who had gone quite pale.

"I'm afraid so."

"I'd be extremely disappointed if Gloria had left him her fortune. I thought she had more sense about her."

All eyes stared at Waverley, waiting to see if he had anything else to add.

"Mr Franks says Gloria had been obsessed with the fact that her daughter had involved herself in some sort of cult. She was determined to find enough evidence about the order to confront her daughter and persuade her to leave, but after Easter died, she went to pieces."

"How awful," said Sarah.

"It is awful. But what if she was still searching for evidence?" said Rachel. "And she found something out, meaning she had to be stopped, just like her daughter?"

"Franks is too upset to speak any further, but he said that Gloria had spent some time with Mother Cross since her daughter's death. Dr Bentley has gone to see Mother Cross to ask whether Gloria had been in touch and what their conversations were about."

"Poor woman. I hope some good comes out of this. I can ask Dad to speak with Connor, if you'd like him to. He and Mum got quite close to them."

"I'll put that to Dr Bentley. It might be helpful, if your father can face another trauma on his cruise."

"Dad deals with life and death all the time. He'll manage," Rachel said. "I hope you don't think this death was natural causes?"

"What do you think?" asked Waverley.

"Two suicides, however plausible the reasoning, during one cruise, both linked in some way to a cultish group with something to hide? No, this is murder."

Chapter 22

Rachel and Marjorie had returned to Marjorie's suite after the meeting with Waverley. He had been too busy and distracted to give them any background on the other nuns under suspicion, or on Abe Cooper. Jason had stayed behind with Waverley so they could plan their next move. Sarah was called to a passenger with a migraine as soon as the meeting was over.

"This really has added confusion to an already muddled case," said Marjorie as she poured a whisky from the small bottles in the fridge for herself. "Drink?"

"Could you open a small red, please?"

With the drinks ready, Rachel rubbed her temples.

"I think we need to go over everything again – as you say, things have become muddled, even in my head."

"Shall I take notes?" Marjorie walked over to the large desk in her room and pulled out a notebook from the drawer.

"Right, we have the death – almost certainly murder – of Easter Balch, formerly Jacintha. Estranged from her mother, in training to be a nun, and recruited by her uncle to look into the holy order that might be up to something as yet unknown. She was unpopular with the nuns, but was that because of her snooping or other reasons?"

"Yes, that's about it on her. I think we'll add the possible fortune-hunting stepfather and some jealous nuns as suspects in her case."

Rachel nodded. "Now, her mother, Gloria Franks, is found dead, her death follows the same pattern as the daughter's, and both are made to look like possible suicides."

"Or accidental death, in Easter's case," suggested Marjorie.

"So if both women were murdered, Connor Franks would be our prime suspect."

"Shall I put him down as such?"

"Yes, for now, although I wonder if the killer wants us to think that. I never like a clear-cut case."

"Okay, but you have to admit he has motive – his wife's fortune. But did he have opportunity? We don't know if he went with his wife to Brimstone Hill Fortress."

"We need to find out if Gloria took any regular medication. The coroner's report will tell us what she died of, but I'm

expecting another digitalis poisoning."
Rachel scratched her head and took a
slurp of wine.

Marjorie paused to take a sip of whisky.
"Then we have the obnoxious Abraham
Cooper. Where does he fit in?"

"Colin Bell suspects him of being up to
something shady and he has a history of
illegal dealings. Colin told me he was also
a bully when he knew him at college.
They were friends for a while, but Colin
didn't want to join in with his
lawbreaking. I agree with Colin: Cooper's
up to something, but what?"

"Do we put him down as a murder
suspect?"

"I wouldn't discount him. He's a nasty
piece of work, a bully and greedy. I think
if he's into anything that would make him
rich, as he implied to the woman he's
with – Colin says that's a business
arrangement rather than a marriage – then

he wouldn't let a young nun stand in his way. The only thing is, I didn't see him up at Brimstone Fortress today, did you?"

"No, I can't say I did, but it was busy with cruise passengers and he could easily have slipped in unnoticed. I suppose we should add the woman he's with to the list of suspects."

Rachel sighed; this was frustrating. "Yep, put her down the bottom for now. We'll need to find out a bit more about her and whether she's travelling under her own name." Taking a deep breath, she continued, "And then there are the nuns."

Marjorie took another drink and frowned. "We still don't know anywhere near enough about them to come up with a motive. Sister Mora Murdoch is not to be trusted, but is that just because she's undermining the Mother Superior to attempt some sort of coup, or is she involved in something more sinister?"

"I don't know anymore. One minute I think she's the key to the whole thing, and the next minute it could be as you say: petty jealousies and ambition. She does set herself apart from Mother Cross and the other older nuns, but the meetings seem to be about some sort of party they're throwing after we leave St Thomas. She was completely separate from the other older nuns up at the pilgrimage site today and passing something to a few of the blue brigade."

Marjorie laughed. "Heretical teachings, I expect."

Rachel took another drink and chuckled. "Could be."

"What do we know about the blessed Blethyn?" asked Marjorie.

"Nothing, other than the fact she seems to crop up everywhere. She follows Mora Murdoch like her life depends on it and has a prickly friendship with Angeline, but is outwardly hostile to those she considers beneath her. That's about my sum of it."

"Those beneath her being poor, frightened Cheryl and Letitia. Now Letitia is a sweet girl, but she also appears besotted with Mora Murdoch. Or is it Mother Cross? I get confused."

"It's Mother Cross she's besotted with, as was Angeline, but today Angeline was with Mora, so the charismatic Sister Murdoch appears to be drawing more of them into her fold."

"Which side do you think Cheryl sits on?"

"Neither. I don't think she belongs at all. I wouldn't be surprised if she leaves the order at the end of the cruise. She knows more than she lets on, though. I'm not sure whether she is genuinely nervous or whether it's all an act to disarm those around her."

"Mm," Marjorie added to her notes.

"In summary, Connor has to be the prime suspect for murder. There's something else going on within the Order of the Blue Light – whether that's illegal or a power struggle, we need to find out. Abraham Cooper, I don't trust – he would be second on the list of suspects, but we also need to find out what it is he's doing on board this ship, because I don't believe for one minute that it's just event management." Rachel drained the wine glass and stood up. "That gives us something to go on, but right now I need some sleep."

"Me too. I had rather a fraught night last night."

"On that subject, promise me you won't leave your room tonight."

Marjorie yawned. "I promise. In fact, I think I'll sleep the sleep of the righteous tonight."

Rachel laughed. "You've been spending too much time around these nuns."

"Not to mention you and your parents."

"Good point. Goodnight, Marjorie." Rachel kissed her friend on the cheek. "Remember to double lock your room."

Marjorie's exasperated sigh could be heard as she closed the door.

Rachel was still bothered about Marjorie being followed and it worried her that her friend could meet with the same end as the other two women. Digitalis drugs were in dangerous hands and whoever had them was not afraid to use them. But the second death was clumsy. She couldn't believe that Connor Franks was stupid enough to drug both Easter Balch and his wife. From what Gloria had said, he'd had no contact with the young woman, who would have snubbed him even if he had gone near her. He had motive, but not opportunity, which brought Abe Cooper back up to the top of her list.

I need to talk to Connor myself and find out where he was at the time of Gloria's death and what his wife had discovered about the religious order. He might know who she spoke to in the days leading to her death.

She called Marjorie from her room and explained her new theory and plan.

"How will you get to speak to him? If he's not guilty, he could be feeling genuinely bereaved."

"You and I will manage it somehow, but we need to be discreet. I don't want anyone seeing us. Perhaps I can get my father involved."

"That is a good idea, Connor and Gloria liked your parents."

"Mm, let's think about it. Marjorie, would you like me to come back and stay the night? I can sleep on the bed settee, I'm sure Mario would make it up for me."

"Not tonight, dear, I'm all locked up and we both need to get some rest. I promise I won't go out."

"And you won't answer the door to anyone?"

Marjorie breathed out a deep sigh. "I won't open the door to anyone. Last night was probably just the overactive imagination of an old lady, and if anyone had been following me, it would have been Blethyn, not an unidentified man. No, I'm satisfied now that it was nothing. I know that Jason didn't see her following me once I was out of the lift."

"Okay, if you're sure. Goodnight again, Marjorie."

"Goodnight, Rachel."
But Rachel wasn't convinced.

Chapter 23

Rachel had no intention of going to bed.
There was more to investigate. She
headed towards the Piano Lounge and sat
out of sight of where Marjorie had told
her she'd been sitting the previous
evening.

Marjorie had described Colin's wife to
her. Rachel wanted to avoid her if she
could, so she called a barman to get her a
drink. Her position was ideal for keeping
an eye on the room without being seen.
Most people looked inwards towards
either the bar or the pianist, whereas she
was sitting on an outer edge close to a
family group. Anyone looking on would
think she was with them, but she wasn't

so close as to intrude. She had a clear view of the table where Abraham Cooper was sitting, this time with the woman who Colin Bell suspected was not his wife. What had Colin said about that relationship? It appeared to be business rather than personal, but Cooper was passing the woman off as his wife.

The woman was middle-aged, apple rather than pear-shaped, with an abdomen bulging through the evening suit, and she was slouching in her chair. They certainly didn't appear intimate, but many couples weren't. The two of them were engaged in a tense conversation, from what Rachel could gather. It was a shame she didn't have Jason's listening device, but the body language told her the woman was not happy. Cooper was gesticulating and shrugging as someone would if saying that something wasn't their fault. Rachel wondered whether this was to do with the death of Gloria Franks, but cautioned herself not to jump to conclusions. It could be unrelated.

Rachel was distracted temporarily by a rowdy crowd of revellers. Complaints from people who were enjoying a pleasant drink reached her ears. The pianist could barely be heard above the commotion, and it wasn't long before Ravanos, a security guard Rachel had met a few times before, entered the bar and encouraged the group to take it elsewhere as they were disturbing the peace. The leader of the group slapped Ravanos on the back in good humour and left the bar. Ravanos noticed Rachel and nodded before leaving.

By the time Rachel turned back to see what Cooper was up to, she was dismayed to see he'd left.

"They've gone." Colin appeared at her side.

"I didn't see you come in," she answered, smiling.

"They didn't want to talk, so I was dismissed. I think they'd had words, perhaps they are married after all." He grinned mischievously.

"They definitely had words, but I was too far away to hear anything. Do you know if either of them met with a woman called Gloria Franks?"

"The woman found dead, you mean? I don't think so. He eats alone in the dining room when he's not with her. Not a very sociable chap, except when sucking up to businessmen. He met with a wealthy guest after dinner this evening."

"What about his pretend wife? Had she met with Gloria Franks?"

Colin shook his head. "No idea, sorry. But Rachel, if you think they're involved in murder, you should speak to the security chief."

"I will. Thanks, Colin. Time I called it a night." With a sigh, she got up from the comfortable seat. "One more thing. Have any of the nuns mentioned Mrs Franks?"

Colin's face contorted into a sceptical frown. "Now you are delving into the realms of fantasy if you think any of them are involved. We were up there watching them today, remember. No, they never mentioned her."

"Yes, they did." A woman appeared behind Rachel. "Colin, you're so forgetful."

Rachel frowned. Perhaps she had got Colin wrong and he was involved.

"This is my wife, Charlene. Charlene, this is Rachel Prince, a friend of Sarah Bradshaw, our favourite nurse, and Jason Goodridge."

"Pleased to meet you!" Charlene beamed. "Your reputation precedes you –

you're our cruise ship sleuth. Are you investigating the suspicious deaths?"

Rachel liked this cheerful woman, who was so much more relaxed than her husband.

"Charlene, those deaths have been ruled probable suicides, as far as I know, and Miss Prince... erm, Rachel is on holiday with her parents, I believe."

"It's good to meet you too, Charlene. Did you say the nuns had mentioned Mrs Franks?"

"Not Mrs, Mr. I heard one of them warn another one to stay away from him. It was on the first night. Don't you remember, Colin?"

"No. My memory isn't what it was. I probably wasn't listening – there was a lot of childish gossip going on that night."

"It was the first meeting that Colin had with his old friend, so he was probably thrown by that. Around six of the young ones were there, as well as the Mother Superior and the grouchy one, Sister Murdoch."

"Where was this?" asked Rachel.

"It was in the Grand Function Room behind the purser's office. I'm sure it was the young girl who died giving the warning, though."

"Do you know who to?"

"Sorry, no. They all looked the same with those blue habits on. The only reason I remember it being the one who died was because she was so dark skinned and she had the most beautiful brown eyes. She also wore lipstick, which none of the others did."

"And you have no idea who she warned off?" Rachel persisted, thinking this could be important.

"No. Are you sure you don't remember, Colin? You were right there. I was serving drinks – nonalcoholic, of course."

"No, I've said already. You probably didn't hear it either. My wife can have a vivid imagination when it comes to ship gossip."

"Oh, really?" Charlene turned on her heel and stormed off.

"Time for me to go, I think. Goodnight, Colin."

Rachel was far less sure than she had been before of Colin's innocence. It now appeared she'd been taken in and he had been fishing for how much she knew. Thoughtful, she returned to her room. Easter Balch and Gloria Franks deserved justice.

"That puts you right back in the frame, Colin Bell," she muttered.

Chapter 24

Susan Prince's head shot up as Rachel arrived for breakfast. "Whatever's the matter, Rachel? You're looking peaky."

"Sorry, Mum, late night," Rachel replied as a waiter pulled out a chair for her to be seated in the Coral Restaurant. She obviously hadn't done a good enough job of disguising her bleary eyes behind her makeup.

"Where's Marjorie this morning?" asked Brendan.

"Having a lie in. I went to collect her, but Mario, her butler, told me she was asleep when he took in her early morning coffee, so he didn't disturb her. I think I might have kept her up too late last night."

"And yourself too, by the looks of you," added her mother, disapproval in her voice.

Rachel ordered coffee and a full English breakfast, lacking energy to fight her mother this morning. They didn't often disagree, but this could be one of those occasions if she wasn't careful. It was important to keep her emotions in check, as it wasn't her mother's fault she felt irritable.

At least they haven't heard about Gloria Franks, she consoled herself. Otherwise that would be the topic, not the state of her eyes.

"You should try to let Marjorie get a little more rest, Rachel," said Brendan. "She's not a young thing like you."

"I will, Dad. We just got talking and the time flew past." Determined not to

352

mention the meeting with Waverley or her excursion to the Piano Lounge, Rachel took a gulp of the coffee that had appeared in front of her. This also drew a disapproving glance from her mother. Rachel sighed and shrugged her shoulders.

"We thought we'd head for the beach today as we haven't booked any tours. Will you be joining us?" Brendan, ever the diplomat, intervened before any further tension could arise.

"I don't think so. I'll let Marjorie sleep for as long as possible, then see what she wants to do. Sarah was on call again last night, so she might also be sleeping. We'll do our own thing and meet you for dinner, if that's okay?"

"Of course, and that's thoughtful of you, Rachel, to let your friends catch up with some rest. It looks beautiful out there."

"It does. I think it's going to be a hot one, so don't forget your sun cream, Mum."

The laughter broke through the tension of moments before. Rachel could see her parents were enjoying their break more and more as each day passed by. Her mother didn't sulk for long generally, unless Rachel stoked the fire, and she had mostly grown out of the temptation to do that.

"Have you heard from Carlos?" asked Brendan.

"No, but as I'm going to have some free time, I think I'll FaceTime him. He was flying back to London yesterday, so should be home by now."

If there had been any further need to soften Rachel's mother, the mention of Carlos did the trick. Susan had been putty in his hands since the first time they met. Must be that Italian charm, Rachel and he joked between themselves. Brendan Prince had taken longer to warm to Carlos after Rachel's previous fiancé had broken her heart and had remained over-protective for some time afterwards. Carlos had also been cautious of Brendan due to his being a parish vicar, but now they got on well and genuinely liked each other.

Rachel glanced around the restaurant as she tucked into her fry up. It was a rarity for her to eat fatty food, as she generally preferred healthy options, but this morning her stomach was grumbling for a fat burst and she wasn't going to deny it. Cooper was sitting in silence with the woman posing as his wife, which made her wonder why the charade? Colin Bell must have had the day off, as he wasn't to be seen. The nuns were at the far end of the restaurant, congregated around four separate tables.

"So much for the silent order I thought they were when they attended Sunday service," said Brendan.

"Yes, it's interesting how they've become noisier and, I think, happier each day since the cruise started. There doesn't appear to be any residual sorrow over the loss of their sister, does there?"

"No, Susan, but perhaps they hide it well. I understand from Gloria that Easter hadn't been a nun very long, so they wouldn't have known her that well."

Rachel tensed at the mention of Gloria's name, which drew a quizzical look from her father, but no comment. She hurriedly concentrated on devouring a sausage with gusto to ensure neither of them would ask her anything about Gloria Franks. Table manners had been instilled into her from an early age, so she could rest assured they wouldn't expect her to speak with her mouth full.

At that moment, her attention was drawn back towards the nuns as raucous laughter erupted from one of the tables. Brendan smiled.

"Perhaps they're not a sect after all. If they can laugh like that, they must be happy. I take back what I said previously about them being too heavenly minded and all that."

Brendan Prince was right. The Order of the Blue Light appeared to be a group of happy young women enjoying a wonderful holiday this morning.

"Perhaps they're allowed to relax now the pilgrimage part of their tour is over, and maybe they feel lightheaded if they were shorn afterwards," Rachel suggested.

"That must be it. I do hope they don't go ahead with repenting of their beauty, though."

"I think they will have done that yesterday, Dad. But they don't seem to be any worse off for it."

After breakfast, Rachel and her parents returned to their deck, and she wished them a pleasant day. "I'll ring you to find out where you are if I get bored," she said as she kissed her mother.

"You do that."

Once in her room, she saw a note had been pushed under the door. It was from Marjorie.

"Sorry, Rachel. I had a bad night and have woken with one of my heads. I'm going to rest up today, but don't you worry, Mario will take care of me. You go out and enjoy yourself. We'll catch up later."

Rachel sighed, feeling guilty that she may have put Marjorie under too much pressure again. It was easy to forget that her friend was in her eighties because she was so sharp witted. Looking in the mirror, she thought it wouldn't be a bad thing to take some time out herself today. She was exhausted, but didn't want to disappoint Sarah, who needed time away from the ship whenever she could get it. She picked up the phone and dialled her friend's room.

"Hello, Rachel, I was just about to call you. Do you mind if we go ashore this afternoon rather than this morning? I've offered to cover surgery for Gwen as an old friend of hers has shown up unexpectedly – apparently taking a holiday on the island and wants to meet up."

"That's not a problem. To be honest, I'm tired so I might just wander around the ship or laze on the balcony for the morning. Marjorie's got a migraine and my parents are heading to the beach."

"Are you sure? I would hate to think you're missing out because of me."

"Perfectly sure. I had a late night and I want to call Carlos anyway."

"Right, I'll ring you on the mobile at lunchtime if you're not in your room."

"Okay, see you later." Rachel returned the phone to its receiver and plonked herself down on the settee after opening the balcony doors wide.

An hour later, she was feeling much more refreshed after speaking with Carlos via FaceTime. They had agreed after her Christmas cruise, when she had been caught up in another murder investigation that ended up with them arguing over her involvement, not to discuss any crimes on board until she returned home. This suited her, because she wouldn't want to hide anything from her fiancé or tread on eggshells when they spoke, especially as he had looked drawn. The family funeral had definitely taken it out of him and she regretted not having been there. He promised he would rest and take a few days off before picking up any new cases. His work as a private investigator was sporadic, but he rarely had gaps where he didn't have an ongoing case, so he had to take them when he could.

Rachel had filled him in on how the medical team were delighted to be invited to the wedding and how much her parents were enjoying their first cruise.

"I think they may have caught the bug."

"They can't afford to," he'd quipped.

After some further banter and lots of phone kisses, the call ended. It always lifted her mood whenever they spoke and she was relieved he would rest up for a few days.

Now it's time for you to head outside, she told herself. She decided to leave the ship and enjoy a solitary walk as she had time before lunch, when she would check up on Marjorie and meet Sarah. Exiting through security with nothing but her cruise card and some US dollars, she took a deep breath of fresh air. The sun immediately beat down on her head as she left the cruise terminal, following a path past crowds of vendors offering to sell her things. Her long mane was tied back in a ponytail and she wore knee-length shorts and a loose grey vest, her valuables in a zipped pocket in her shorts.

The island of St Lucia was exotic and inviting, despite the bustling of locals and tourists. After walking for some time in a daze, she realised she had veered off the main paths and into a secluded narrow road where she could no longer hear the noise of traffic or voices. The beach was in sight, so heeding warnings that tourists could be a target for criminals, she headed towards it.

Her footsteps were silent due to her soft sandals and the road had become eerily quiet. Her heart rate quickened along with her breathing as the familiar adrenaline that accompanied danger surged through her body.

Idiot, Prince. Why didn't you stick to the main paths?

Hearing footsteps behind her, she decided to turn to get a look at what she was facing before making her next move. She saw a brute of a man heading towards her, wielding a flick knife.

You've got to be kidding. I'm not fighting him.

She turned back and ran towards the beach, only to be confronted by two other men who appeared from nowhere just ahead of her. Her heart was now racing at zillions of beats per minute and panic made her freeze to the spot. Even with her self-defence and karate training, it was going to be difficult to take on three men with knives, especially as the one behind her was built like a hippopotamus.

Trying to calm her trembling body enough to at least put up some resistance, she started to walk slowly towards the two men ahead of her, who were standing still. She could hear the brute behind closing in and breathing heavily, so she assessed he wasn't that fit.

Doesn't need to be at that size, she thought hysterically, almost chuckling to herself.

She reached the spot where the two men were blocking her path. One of them smirked through gapped teeth. The second man, dressed in shorts and black vest showing huge biceps from frequent workouts, did not move, speak nor smile. This was worse than the lecherous grin on the other guy's face, warning Rachel that he was the more dangerous. She stared at the second man, realising the third was now inches behind her.

"Excuse me, I need to get past." Her voice was as controlled as she could get it to be.

"Are you Rachel Prince?" the unsmiling man said.

Now Rachel shook with fear. This wasn't just a random mugging; this could be a hit.

"Why do you want to know?"

She felt the brute's arms grab hers from behind while Straight-face nodded to Lech, who went for her. Her knee was up in an instant, instinctively catching him in the groin, and he dropped to the floor, screaming in pain. Brute held her tighter, causing pain to rip through her shoulders.

"Are you going to fight any more?" Straight-face asked.

"It depends what you have in mind," she grimaced and stuttered through the pain.

"I just want to check who you are, seeing as you're not being helpful." He reached his hand towards her zipped pocket.

"Okay, I'm Rachel Prince. What do you want?"

Straight-face nodded to Brute, who released her. Lech was rolling around on the ground. Could she take the other two on and come out alive? Of this she wasn't certain. If only she had a truncheon or taser.

"Someone wants you dead. Do you know Jason Goodridge?"

"Of course, and I don't believe for one minute that Jason wants me dead, so why don't you crawl back into whatever hole you came out of? Unless you're going to tell me what this is all about."

Straight-face smiled for the first time. "He told me you have guts. You're right, it's not Jason. We were hired this morning through a third party to take you out. We do some mercenary work on the island. Pays the bills when you get dumped by the army. We were given a photo and followed you off the ship. Rolo here bumped into Jason – our paths crossed in Afghanistan – and they got talking. Lucky for you Rolo can't keep his gob shut – likes to brag." The sarcasm in his voice didn't escape Rolo, who was living up to his name, still rolling around on the ground.

"Wish I hadn't now I've met you," he groaned.

"Anyway, we owe Jason, so when he says that we are not to touch you, we don't."

"What about your employer?" she snapped. "Who is he?"

"Don't know, and even if we did, we wouldn't say. Loyalty only goes so far. Anyway, we thought we'd warn you that someone's after you. Someone who can splash the cash, if you know what I mean. You've really annoyed someone, Rachel Prince, so if I were you, I'd try to be a little nicer."

"I'll take it under advisement. Now, am I free to go?"

Straight-face stood aside and let her pass. She would have liked to have found out who was paying these men, but didn't want to take any more chances in case they decided money was more important than whatever favour they owed Jason.

Thank you, Lord. She fired up a quick prayer as she headed back to the ship at a jog.

Chapter 25

The relief on Waverley's face when Rachel passed through security was clear. He nodded her through the metal detector, unable to speak, but the eye contact between them said so much more than words. Rachel headed towards the stairs as the chief of security waved the next passenger through. She ran up them to release more of the adrenaline that threatened to overwhelm her, taking thirteen sets with ease.

Rachel unlocked her room and threw herself down on the bed, sucking in deep breaths caused by the run and the terror of the near-miss. After taking a shower and calling for and drinking down a pot of coffee, she felt normal again. Now her legs no longer felt like they were going to collapse from under her, it was time to call on Marjorie.

Marjorie answered her door immediately, dressed and well-groomed as ever.

"Hello, dear. I did call your room, but there was no reply, so I assumed you were out with Sarah and your parents. Rachel, are you all right?"

Rachel nodded, realising she must still appear pasty. "I'm fine now. Had a bit of a fraught morning. I'll tell you about it soon, but I said I'd meet Sarah for lunch. Are you up to it?"

"Yes, I am. I thought I was going to get one of those wretched migraines, but I caught it early. A couple of Migraleve tablets and I feel absolutely fine. Let's meet Sarah. You can tell me about your adventure over a meal. Did you go out with your parents?"

"No, I just went for a walk." Rachel's mobile rang. "Hi, Sarah. Yes, I'm back. Marjorie's with me; shall we meet in the buffet? Okay, see you in ten minutes."

"I'll just get my handbag," said Marjorie.

Rachel's legs felt weak from running up thirteen flights of stairs, so she was pleased the buffet was only a deck away. It was difficult to believe that everything continued as normal when she had experienced such a close call with death that – had it not been for Jason – could have turned out so differently. Watching people gaily gathering mountains of food on to trays made her want to yell, but she took some deep breaths and controlled her emotions, just as she had done when confronted by her would-be attackers.

This time, she opted for a healthy salad and a bowl of fruit for lunch. Marjorie didn't enjoy buffet food, but was being well catered for by one of the waiters who offered to take her round and carry her tray. Rachel found a table and waved to her white-haired friend and the willing waiter. Marjorie slipped him a few dollars and took her seat.

"The crew on board are always so helpful to a frail old lady."

"Less of the frail old lady business with me," laughed Rachel. "That's a healthy chunk of food you've got there, considering you're slumming it."

"Ah well, I went without breakfast, you see. Us frail old ladies need to keep our strength up if we're going to hang around with you youngsters."

Rachel enjoyed the friendly banter and appreciated Marjorie not asking about her morning. Like all good friends, she would wait for the right opportunity.

Sarah arrived with a tray laden with food that put Marjorie's to shame.

"What? I missed breakfast."

"I didn't say anything," Rachel protested.

"The dropped jaw said it all," answered Sarah, eyes rolling. "Hello, Marjorie, are you feeling better?"

"I am, thank you. Caught it before it took hold. Don't worry about the guinea pig over there, I got a look too when I arrived with a full plate."

Rachel smiled. "I did have a full English this morning, if that makes you feel any better."

"It does," quipped Sarah, tucking into a healthy portion of lasagne.

"How was your morning?" Marjorie asked Sarah. "I thought you were supposed to be off today."

"I am now, but I covered for Gwen this morning as an old friend is staying on the island and wanted to meet up with her. Did you do anything, Rachel?"

Rachel drew in a deep breath, exhaling slowly before explaining about her walk and getting drawn away from the crowds into a quiet road.

Sarah gasped. "Rachel, please don't tell me you were mugged."

"Worse."

Rachel continued the story, relating how the three men had taken her unawares and trapped her. Sarah paled and put down her fork; Marjorie listened intently.

"Well, you're here without a scratch, so I'm assuming you got the better of them. Are they lying in an alley somewhere?" Marjorie's attempt at humour had the desired effect as colour returned to Sarah's face and Rachel smiled.

"Not quite, although I did manage to curb a man called Rolo's love life for a few weeks, I expect."

Marjorie's eyes twinkled. "Oh I would have enjoyed seeing that, but how did you get away?"

"They let me go, thanks to Jason."

Sarah's head shot up. "Did Jason rescue you?"

"Not physically, but yes. It seems he ran into the one who I put out of action for a while, who seemingly bragged about being on a job. Jason discovered they were after me and managed to persuade him to tell the others to let me be. Seems they owed him a favour. I think they were expats who served with Jason at some time in the past. I haven't managed to see him to thank him yet, but I owe him."

"Oh Rachel, who's got it in for you this time? Did you find out?"

"No, they either didn't know or weren't saying, but someone paid them and I intend to find out who."

"We've been so discreet," said Marjorie. "I don't know how anyone could want to have you killed, and I really can't imagine any of the nuns being able to hire hitmen. It doesn't bear thinking about. It has to be Franks. I've suspected him all along."

"But why would he want to harm Rachel?" asked Sarah. "He barely knows her."

"He must have found out who she is – you know how loose tongues on board a ship can be more than anyone, Sarah. Perhaps he thinks she saw something at Brimstone Hill Fortress. Remember Colin Bell saw her, so Franks could have done too."

"Good point. Yes, while we were looking around on the flat, he could have followed her. Although we don't know if he was up there at all. I certainly didn't see him."

"Excuse me, you two, I am here, you know!"

They laughed as they finished their meals, but Rachel knew that Sarah would not relax until whoever had hired the men was caught and locked up. For that matter, neither would she.

"You won't want to go ashore this afternoon, I suppose." Sarah sounded disappointed.

"No, you must stay on board, Rachel," added Marjorie.

"I have every intention of going ashore. I will not have my life controlled by people who think they can scare me. Anyway, those guys won't come near us again. They'll stay hidden."

"What makes you so sure?" asked Sarah.

"Because they will be arrested by the security team if they show their faces now Waverley knows I'm safe – you should have seen the relief on his face when I returned unscathed, I wish I'd had a camera – and whoever paid them will want their money back or worse, so we're safe. Besides, I'll be with you two and we can meet my parents. They're down there somewhere."

"All right. As long as you promise to stay with us at all times. We'll just go for a walk along the beach and grab a drink with Brendan and Susan," Marjorie insisted.

"Deal," said Rachel, laughing. "I think I'd have come out on top in a fight anyway."

"Not from what you said about the one you called Brute, he sounds like the Hulk to me." Sarah shot her a look and raised her eyebrows.

Rachel did a mock brow wipe. "It's a good thing we don't need to find out. I'll put it down to a lapse in judgement. If I hadn't been thinking about the two deaths, I probably wouldn't have strayed off the main paths at all. I'm an idiot sometimes and probably lucky they were hired thugs rather than real muggers. I read all the warnings, so it would have been my fault if I had been mugged."

"Let's not go there," said Sarah. "I can't think about what might have happened, it's bad enough dealing with what has."

"Quite right. Now come along, you two young things. This old lady wants to explore the island of St Lucia before anyone else gets killed."

"You've got a wicked sense of humour sometimes, Lady Marjorie Snellthorpe," said Rachel, taking her arm.

Chapter 26

Rachel and Marjorie sat on the older woman's balcony, taking in the smell of the sea again as the ship set sail from St Lucia towards its penultimate destination, the island of Antigua. It had been quite a cruise thus far and Rachel would be in no hurry to return to St Lucia again, even though her terrifying experience hadn't been anything to do with the island. Thugs and hired hands could be found all over the world, including in England.

"Your parents seem to be having an amazing time. I take it they don't know about Gloria Franks?"

"No, I haven't had the heart to tell them. They are so happy; it wouldn't be right. I'm not going to ask Dad to speak to Connor. Let Waverley handle him."

"That's a good idea. Have you decided it was Connor Franks after all?" asked Marjorie.

"I haven't come to any conclusions. To be honest, Marjorie, I've had enough of murder and mayhem for now. I don't know what it would do to Carlos if something happened to me, and seeing my parents this afternoon, laughing and joking, all I could think was what if I had been found dead in that alley?"

"I agree with you, Rachel. But you are who you are, and although I tremble at the thought of anything happening to you, I wouldn't want to change you in any way. It's quite natural to think like that after such a close encounter."

Rachel knew Marjorie was right, but didn't really want to hear it right now. All she wanted was to disengage from the sense of duty she felt about finding out who'd killed Easter Balch and Gloria Franks. Of course, she would very much like to know who wanted to kill her, too, if only to protect Marjorie and her parents from being caught in the crossfire. There was no escape and she knew it. Whoever it was had her in their sights, when they found out she was still alive, they would no doubt try again.

"What I don't understand is why? I've kept a relatively low profile, and as you say, it's not likely any of the nuns would know men like those I came across today, let alone want to pay them to attack me. It has to be something to do with Connor Franks, unless—"

"Unless what, dear?"

"Unless it's someone else linked to the nuns. Colin Bell, for instance."

"I thought we'd ruled him out."

"We had, but after I left you last night, I couldn't resist going down to the Piano Lounge myself."

The flicker of a frown crossed Marjorie's face, only to be replaced with curiosity.

"Nothing happened, apart from Cooper and his pretend wife having an argument, but Colin joined me. When I asked if any of the nuns had mentioned Gloria Franks, he denied it, but his wife overheard us talking."

"Charlene?"

"Yes. She said there had been a drinks reception or something on the first night and that Easter had warned one of the nuns against having any contact with him."

"You mean Connor Franks?"

"Yes. Charlene was certain that Colin must have heard something, but he vehemently denied it, then insulted his wife, implying she made things up. He was quite aggressive. So, you see, if he does have anything to do with these deaths, or some shady dealings with the religious order – we know he has reignited a friendship with the horrible Abe Cooper – he could have had something to do with the hired hands today. In fact, the more I think of it, the more it points to him."

"He denies being friends with Cooper, though, doesn't he? And I can't see him having the money to hire such people. Hits cost a lot of money, if I remember from my one and only oh-so-close experience of such things. There was a hefty price on my head."

Rachel took Marjorie's hands in earnest. "We're both lucky to be here."

"I thought you would say divine intervention."

"Definitely that as well. Back to Colin, though. He could be earning big money if he's got himself mixed up in something worth taking the risk. We don't know what it is yet or how much money's involved, but we do know that it may have cost two lives, almost three."

"I don't have Colin down as someone who would associate themselves with such people. He's such a good maître d."

"In that case, he can't *possibly* be the murderer, Marjorie." They both giggled at the absurdity of what Marjorie had just said.

"Come on, it's time to go see the chief of security. I told my parents you so enjoyed the buffet at lunchtime, you wanted to eat there again tonight."

Marjorie thumped her on the arm. "It will have to be select dining this evening, then. Under no circumstances am I going to eat in a buffet twice in one day. I suggest we go to the steak restaurant afterwards."

"You are such a snob sometimes, Lady Marjorie," Rachel said as she pulled her friend up from a chair on the balcony and took one more look at the small boats racing to keep up with the gigantic *Coral Queen* as she sailed to her next destination.

Waverley was in his office when they arrived and summoned them in with a wave of the hand. He was alone, but the bounce in his step was a giveaway that he had good news.

"Please take a seat, ladies; we're just waiting for Goodridge. It's good to see you in one piece, Rachel. When Goodridge told me you were in danger, I was all for calling in the local police, but he convinced me the men would do as he asked. I didn't feel at all comfortable about it until I witnessed your safe return myself."

"What I can't understand is why Jason didn't accompany the man called Rolo to make sure Rachel was safe," said Marjorie.

"He was going to, but by the time he'd called me to explain what he wanted to do, the man had done a bunk. He had already given him the leader's telephone number, though, so Goodridge called him to make sure the message was loud and clear. Seems they owed our security officer a debt of honour, not that these men sound honourable. I did give Goodridge permission to go after them, and he was still searching when you returned to the ship, Rachel. So, can I get you ladies a drink?"

"Oh, I'll have a glass of your wonderful Scotch," said Marjorie. "The whisky in my room just doesn't have the same quality."

Waverley obliged by going to his drinks cabinet. "And for you, Rachel?"

"Do you have any martini? Martini and lemonade's my drink."

"I don't have any, but I'll phone down for one now and get a bottle in for the future. Goodridge will want a tonic water; what about Sarah?"

Rachel hadn't realised Sarah would be joining them, but she was pleased. "Sarah likes white wine usually, although she has red for my sake as I'm not a fan."

"White wine it is, then." Waverley picked up the phone and called down for Rachel's martini, then prepared the rest of the drinks. He hummed as he worked, resulting in a raise of the eyebrows from Marjorie.

"I take it you have good news?" Rachel jumped in before Marjorie became impatient, although she seemed happy to savour a generous glass of fine Scotch.

"We have him – the killer – in the brig." Waverley's smug grin brought a smile to Rachel's face.

"Him?" she quizzed.

"Franks?"

"How did you know, Lady Snellthorpe... erm, Marjorie? I only put it all together today."

Jason arrived with Sarah before Marjorie could respond. A waiter arrived simultaneously, and Jason took Rachel's drink and handed it to her.

"I assume this is yours," he said, grinning. The couple joined Rachel and Marjorie as Waverley prowled around like a peacock in full plume.

"I was just telling Rachel and Marjorie about the arrest, Goodridge, but I think

Rachel would like you to fill her in on your, erm, acquaintances."

Jason smiled sheepishly at Rachel. "Glad you're okay; today could have been nasty. There's not a lot to be said, other than Rolo likes to brag – something I'm pleased about for once. I saw him at the gates looking suspicious and recognised him straight away. He's all brawn and no brains. I knew he and the other guys worked as hired thugs, so I went over to warn him off if he was scouting any of our passengers. It turned out he was waiting for the money, while Big Den and Ice were on your tail."

"Big Den due to his size, and Ice because he is—"

"A cold-blooded killer, but on this occasion, they were only being paid to rough you up."

"Only?" shouted Sarah. "I think that's bad enough, don't you?"

"Sorry, I just meant—"

"But he told me someone wanted me dead," Rachel intervened before Sarah and Jason could carry on arguing.

"Did he? That's just mouth. No, their orders were to rough you up so you couldn't do any more snooping. Ice always was prone to exaggeration. He was trying to scare you; it's his way. He actually enjoys violence."

"Well he succeeded in scaring me, although I don't think Rolo will be exercising his manhood for a while."

Jason smiled. "I warned them you were tough."

"This is not a game, you two," said Sarah, exasperated. "Rachel could have been seriously hurt."

"Sarah's right," agreed Marjorie.

"Sorry," said Rachel. "To be honest, I was frightened. My mind went into overdrive trying to work out whether I could escape, but your Big Den had me in a vicelike grip. Those men can't be friends of yours, Jason."

"They're not. I don't like any of them, but when you're in the army, you're a team. I saved them from a suicide bomber once. They were about to approach him all gung-ho, but I could see the trigger, so shot him before they got close enough for him to detonate."

Sarah frowned, obviously not wanting to hear about the man she loved killing people.

"Perhaps it would have been better for the world if you had let them all explode, by the sounds of it," Marjorie suggested.

"If I'd known what they would become, I might have been tempted, but you can't make those decisions in the heat of battle. Not that I could have done that anyway. We needed each other. That's the way it was."

"On to more pleasant topics: how do you know it was Connor who hired these men?" asked Rachel.

"Ah," said Waverley, pleased it was his turn for the limelight, "I asked for security footage of the gates and we saw Franks meeting with the man named Rolo and taking something from him. It has to be about Mrs Franks's money. We interviewed him about his whereabouts yesterday. He originally told us he didn't go to Brimstone Hill Fortress at all, tried to say he and Gloria had been on separate outings. I showed him evidence of the two of them leaving the ship together, and both getting into a taxi. The taxi firm confirms they were taken to Brimstone Hill; the driver remembered Franks's South African accent and thought the woman was Franks's mother, but it was them."

"Ah, that's his real accent. I knew the posh American one was a fake," Rachel interrupted.

Waverley's brow furrowed, but he nodded and continued his story. "When I challenged him with these facts, he changed his story – said they did go together, that they had a row about her obsession with her daughter and he returned to the ship alone. The only truth in that story, of course, is that he returned to the ship alone."

Waverley finally sat down and took a sip of his own Scotch. He rubbed his trousers with the self-satisfied excitement of a child.

"And what did he say about paying Rolo? I prefer my name for him: Lech."

"He denies it, of course; says he has no idea what I'm talking about, but he'll crack eventually."

"Does he even know who I am?" asked Rachel. "It was my parents he spoke to mostly."

"He admits to noticing you because of your, erm, looks. That's all."

"Hmm." Rachel was thoughtful. Something about this story didn't ring true for her, but the facts did point to Connor Franks being the guilty party, especially as he'd had the opportunity to kill his wife while they were out. "How did he get to Easter? She wouldn't have had anything to do with him."

"I think he must have tracked her down and slipped something into her drink that morning at breakfast before church. We haven't got proof of that yet, but I'm sure he'll see sense before too long. The other evidence is enough to get him for the murder of his wife and for paying the thugs to attack you."

Rachel felt the evidence was spurious, but now might not be the time to go on the attack. Waverley could jump to conclusions to tie up a case, but to his credit would always concede that he was wrong if evidence led elsewhere.

"Do you know how he got hold of digitalis? I assume that was what was given to Gloria as well."

"Gloria Franks was injected with the stuff, so would have died quicker than her daughter, which was a kindness. But yes, I think we know – he was a chemist before he married Gloria Franks."

Marjorie's head shot up. "A chemist? You've spoken to the man! If he's a chemist, I'm a rocket scientist. That man's a gigolo if ever I saw one, nothing more."

Waverley coughed for the first time during the meeting, clearly uncomfortable that he may have been misled.

"His records have him down as a chemist."

He rubbed his hand through the remains of his hair. Rachel felt sorry for him.

"He may have lied to impress, I'm afraid," she said. "Unless he bought the qualification, I think Marjorie's right: he didn't know what digitalis or diazepam were when we spoke to him and Gloria. My father suggested she might need something to help her relax after we delivered the bad news. No chemist would not know what diazepam was."

"And if he didn't know what digitalis was, how could he know how much to give to kill someone or how to inject it?" asked Sarah.

"If he lied about being a chemist, he could equally have been lying about his knowledge of drugs. Let's face it, there aren't many people who haven't heard of diazepam. Maybe he was trying to distance himself from any such knowledge. None of this proves anything. He must have researched poisons and opted for digitalis as a murder weapon."

"No, but if he isn't a chemist, it does make it harder to prove his guilt with the circumstantial evidence we have at present and no idea how he got access to digitalis, plus a syringe and needle, to kill his wife."

"Are you saying he's not the murderer, Rachel?" asked Sarah, biting her bottom lip as she did when stressed.

"I agree that the motive points to him, but I don't think there's enough proof to get him convicted. I take it he was the heir to Gloria Franks's fortune?" asked Rachel.

"Yes, he was," said Waverley. "We'll get the proof. The man's almost ready to confess, don't worry. We have the right man."

Rachel nodded and got up slowly.

"Marjorie and I need to eat; it's been a long day. Would you excuse us?"

"Of course. And I mean it, Rachel. Don't worry. He's our man," said Waverley.

The thing was, Rachel was worried. Very worried.

Chapter 27

Marjorie shook her head. "Buffoon of a man! When will he ever learn? He goes around like a runaway train, slamming into anything that gets in the way. How could he think Connor Franks is a chemist? It's preposterous."

Rachel was deep in thought, so she let Marjorie rant. She could see how it would be easy to suspect Connor Franks of murdering his wife for her money. He might also have stretched to murdering his stepdaughter if she was first in line for inheritance, but why would he want Rachel beaten up? If it was about the conversation she'd had with Colin Bell the previous evening, then he was implicated too. Colin must have told Connor about it.

"Rachel?" Marjorie was looking at her.

"Sorry, I was thinking."

"Yes, I can see that, but you'll be better thinking with some food inside you. The lady here has just asked if we would like a table by the window."

"Yes please, that would be perfect."

Rachel didn't feel hungry when she sat down, but by the time the aroma of steak filtered through, she couldn't believe how quickly she devoured a wonderfully cooked medium-rare fillet. The Beaujolais helped it go down nicely and she felt much better as she looked out at the starry night.

"Thank you, Marjorie."

Marjorie had insisted on picking up the tab for the meal supplement that was required for speciality dining on board the *Coral*. Rachel hadn't had time to remove her cruise card from her purse before Marjorie had handed hers to the waiter.

"Although Waverley can be brash sometimes, and for all the circumstantial evidence, it doesn't mean he hasn't got the right man, you know," Marjorie said.

"That's true. I just wish he'd waited a while, because we could have tracked Connor and done some more digging before throwing him in the brig. It's all about evidence."

"Now I think about it, I believe Waverley's overreacted to protect you. He's very fond of you, and I can forgive him for the rush if that's why he did it."

Rachel twirled her engagement ring. The security of her relationship with Carlos helped her think.

"Oh dear, I think you're right, but that doesn't help us nail Connor Franks as the killer. I realise everything points his way, but he doesn't seem the type to kill people or have women beaten up. If, as you say, he's a gigolo, he's all about charm and courtship. He may well have been after Gloria's money, but I think he was genuinely fond of her. I'm not sure he loved her – only he knows that – but they were good together. I still can't think how he could get close enough to Easter to kill her. You heard what her mother said."

"So who do you think it was if it wasn't him?"

"It would make more sense for there to be two murderers were it not for the use of the same drug and the relationship between the two women, so it has to be one. I was convinced it was one of the nuns who killed Easter Balch. We've also got Abe Cooper, who is involved in this somehow, and now I believe Colin Bell is wrapped up in it. He's the only one who knows who I am and that I've investigated murders on board ship before. His wife told me she knew of me by reputation. The only way someone could have tied me to this case is through a crew member."

"Such a shame. I like Colin, but if he is involved, we need to prove it. I don't think the nuns are involved in the murder of Gloria Franks; they wouldn't have known her, so by the process of elimination, they can't have killed Easter either. What's our next move?"

"We assume Franks is guilty, but just in case, we need backgrounds on all those people we listed as suspects last night. Have you still got your notes? Let's find Jason and see if we can get access. There's bound to be something that links someone to these murders, and as I don't fancy being a target again, it's time to go on the offensive."

"I can't, Rachel; it's more than my job's worth. The boss will go mad. Backgrounds, yep, I agree to, but not this."

"How important is it?" asked Sarah.

"Extremely. I wouldn't be asking if it weren't."

"But you're asking me to break the rules. I can't do it."

"Is there any other way I can speak to him? Is Waverley due any time off?"

"Not tomorrow, but he does have the day off when we get to St Thomas. He and Brenda are going snorkelling. Another way is to get a phone to Franks. I suppose I could let him have it to call a lawyer and monitor him doing that. It wouldn't be impossible for you to get his number and give him a call while he has the phone."

Rachel grinned. "That might be a plan if I need to speak to him before we get to St Thomas. Let's do background checks first and see what they throw up."

The four made their way to Marjorie's suite as it was the largest room and Jason pulled out his laptop. He signed in through the layers of security to bring up passenger details while Marjorie ordered coffees all round. Sarah was quiet, showing signs of anxiety. Rachel knew her friend hated breaking the rules, but would do anything to ensure that she and Marjorie remained safe. She put her arm around her.

"We'll find out who's responsible for these murders and who wants me roughed up. Remember it could still be Connor Franks, and he's safely locked away."

Sarah brightened. "You're right. I do hope it is him."

Rachel squeezed her friend's hand, appreciating how difficult this was for her. "Thank you for being my best friend."

Rachel couldn't help but feel exceptionally lucky to have such good friends as the three people here with her tonight. The warm evening air felt good and the comforting sound of the sea created a calm she didn't feel on the inside.

Marjorie joined them on the balcony. There was no danger of their conversation being overheard, as the balcony was attached to one of two large suites at the stern. The other suite was on the starboard side and separated from them by a huge chunk of maritime architecture.

"Right, I'm in," said Jason, joining them on the balcony with his laptop. "Where do you want to start? Remember we have limited information, but we can certainly access some personal details, including any previous. If we need anything else, the boss will have to request that from Stateside."

"Understood," said Rachel. "Start with the two dead women."

There was nothing significant in Gloria Franks's files, and Easter Balch's record was sparse. She went to college in New York before joining the holy order. As Dr Bentley had already informed them, she listed her next of kin as her uncle, Duncan Rodrigues. The telephone number was unobtainable, but the team now knew this was Detective Rodrigues of the NYPD.

The searches on the Order of the Blue Light turned out to be fruitless. All they learned was where each nun went to college or university, who they were travelling with and next of kin. The records were more concerned with health insurance than with any sensible history.

Even Abraham Cooper's record was banal and turned up nothing. His travelling companion was Esther Jordan, a forty-four-year-old woman listed as a business manager/director. Her next of kin was Pamela Jordan, daughter.

"I wonder why they're posing as husband and wife. People refer to them as Mr and Mrs Cooper," Rachel observed.

"The travel documents list them separately, though, and they are in a twin room, according to the record, so maybe they're just playing along rather than taking the time to explain what is, after all, none of our business," suggested Sarah.

"They could be having an affair," said Marjorie.

"Why the twin beds then?"

"I don't think any of this is relevant to our investigation, so perhaps we should move on."

"You're right, Jason. In fact, I don't think we're any wiser now than we were before. We need more detail, which means we have to ask Waverley," Rachel groaned. "I thought he would have done background checks on Abe Cooper at least."

"Don't give up; we haven't looked at Mora Murdoch or Mother Cross yet." Sarah seemed to be getting into the search now, despite her misgivings earlier.

"Here we are, Priscilla Cross, Mother Superior of the Order of the Blue Light. Nun for fifty years, nothing else to say." Jason moved to flick to the next person.

"Hang on. Look there!" Rachel pointed to the screen and all mouths dropped open.

"So the Mother Superior has her own secret to hide," said Marjorie.

Rachel stared again at the screen. Next of kin: Jessica Rodrigues, daughter. Now things were beginning to make sense.

"How is this significant?" Sarah asked. "Lots of people had children out of wedlock even back then."

"Its only significance is that she has kept it secret, Sarah; she's been lying all these years and probably joined a convent dishonestly. The question is, did Easter know about this from her uncle, or did she find out for herself and try a little blackmail?"

"A Mother Superior wouldn't want the order to know about a secret love child, would she? Do you suspect Detective Rodrigues is Jessica's half-brother?" asked Marjorie.

"Yes, I do, and Duncan Rodrigues must be younger than Jessica. As they have the same surname, it must have been his father who had a relationship with the young Priscilla Cross and, when she felt the calling to become a nun, she left the child with him.

"And if you remember, Angeline complained about how close the new girl – Easter – was to Mother Cross. We know she was on a secret mission on behalf of Uncle Duncan – perhaps it was to make contact with his half-sister's mother? Who knows, maybe it was Jessica that asked him to find her mother?" Rachel was beginning to get a clearer picture. "Either Easter Balch was a messenger or a blackmailer. The other nuns did complain she was always asking questions."

"I still don't see why Mother Cross would harm Easter Balch either way. She's a devout woman, from what we can see," said Jason. "Let's take a look at the other one, Mora Murdoch."

Sister Murdoch was seventy-two, previous foreign language teacher from La Presa, California. She had been a nun for forty-two years and her next of kin was listed as a brother.

"No love child there, then. I would have preferred it to have been her," said Marjorie.

"Let's call it a night. I think we've got as far as we can with this," said Jason. "Come on, Sarah, I'll walk you home," he grinned.

After Sarah and Jason had left, Marjorie poured herself another coffee. Rachel stood up and peered over the balcony rail at the dark sea beneath them. As the ship trundled along at an even pace, everything appeared peaceful. No-one knew what was really going on in the thousands of staterooms neatly arranged throughout the ship, or within the crew quarters. Each person or unit was only aware of their own portion of the world, enjoying spectacular views, luxurious surroundings and a plethora of entertainments to leave them with a memorable experience. For two women, though, the journey had been their final voyage. Rachel looked up at the stars and felt tears trailing down her cheeks.

Chapter 28

There hadn't been any time for more investigations after the meeting broke up in Marjorie's room the night before. Sarah and Jason were working all day, and Sarah was now on call. Rachel had booked on-shore activities for herself and her father to do while Marjorie and Susan watched on.

Rachel had to admit she thoroughly enjoyed going snorkelling with her father. He was like a child, brimming with excitement the whole time they were being taught how to use the sea scooter. Rachel was thrilled to see him so happy, as was her mother judging by the ever present grin plastered on Susan's face.

After the lesson, Rachel and Brendan were kitted out with life vest, flippers, goggles and snorkel. They each grabbed a sea scooter and waved to Marjorie and Susan before entering the crystal-clear water. Rachel had never seen water like it; it was beautiful. They swam with turtles and Brendan gesticulated and pointed the whole time, almost letting go of his scooter twice.

The day in Antigua had passed quickly. Rachel's parents called it a night after dinner. Marjorie and Rachel sat in the main atrium, listening to a string quartet.

"On a day like today, it's easy to forget about our murder investigation, isn't it?" said Marjorie.

"That has to be one of the best days out I've ever had. How often do we get to see turtles in the wild? The weather and storms might be brutal in the Caribbean at times, but the waters and wildlife make up for it. Did you see Dad's face when he came out of the water?"

"You're never too old to enjoy life, Rachel. Remember that. I would have liked a go myself – stupid rules saying I'm too old."

"You didn't bring your swimming kit." Rachel nudged her playfully.

"Well, that is true. Still, while you were frolicking in the sea, I was actually giving serious thought to our murders. I don't believe Franks did kill his wife after all."

"Oh?"

"I saw a couple on the beach today and they looked so happy, and I remember seeing that look in Connor's eyes before Easter Balch collapsed. I don't know whether you remember, but I was speaking to him before the unfortunate event in the chapel. When he saw how distressed his wife was, he was beside himself. I don't think you could act that one. A chemist he may not be, but after reflecting on that fateful morning during the church service, I do think he loved his wife."

"So we're back to finding out who it could have been. I left a note for Waverley this morning, requesting thorough background checks on Cheryl, Angeline, Letitia, Blethyn and the Mother Superior. Jason was going to suggest the same for Abraham Cooper and Mrs Jordan."

"Let's hope the man gets on with it rather than digging his heels in. You know what he can be like."

"I feel like I know who it is, but can't quite pull it all together just yet."

"What's holding you back?"

"Motive for the second killing and the attack on me, but that's another thing – the two things don't add up." She took a deep breath.

Marjorie nudged Rachel as the younger nuns from their art class table approached. Theirs was the only place where there were vacant seats.

"Do you mind if we join you?" asked Letitia brightly.

"Not at all. Go ahead," said Rachel.

The four women appeared relaxed, happier since the pilgrimage was behind them. Even Angeline smiled at Rachel and Marjorie, although Blethyn ignored them, speaking only to Letitia next to her.

"Are you enjoying the rest of your holiday?" asked Marjorie.

"I am," said Cheryl, casting an anxious glance around for fear of anyone hearing her say she was enjoying herself. "We went to the beach today, although the sisters disapproved."

"You mean Sister Murdoch," said Letitia, ignoring Blethyn's glare and giggling.

"That's not fair," said Angeline. "She only wants the best for us. These worldly pleasures are all passing temptations. We're called to higher things."

"Like when you were talking to that blonde, you mean?" Blethyn snapped.

Angeline reddened. "What are you suggesting?"

Rachel felt the young woman's discomfort and intervened. "We went snorkelling. My father was like a child, going all gooey over the turtles."

"The waters were beautiful, weren't they?" said Cheryl. "I felt like I was missing out somehow wearing all this gear."

The three other nuns crossed themselves. "Cheryl, what is it with you? One minute you're in, the next you're out," Letitia teased while Blethyn scowled.

"Isn't that what being a noviciate is all about?" said Marjorie. "Deciding whether taking holy orders is right for you?"

"It is about that, yes. And I'm thinking of going back to college in New York," Cheryl said haughtily. "I don't agree with some of the stuff that goes on in this order. I'm sick of being told what to do by people who think they are better than me." She glared at Blethyn and Angeline in turn before looking back to Marjorie. Rachel noticed her hands had stopped trembling. "Some people think they are high and mighty when really they're nothing. If I do decide to stay, Sister Murdoch reckons I'll make a better nun than the lot of them."

Blethyn's face went scarlet as she gripped the arms of the chair. "Take that back! You know it's not true. You'll never make a good nun, you tell too many lies for one."

"At least I don't pretend to be something I'm not," Cheryl sneered, looking at Angeline again.

The bickering continued for another fifteen minutes while the string quartet took a break. The only one who seemed uncomfortable with the behaviour was Letitia, who was trying unsuccessfully to bring peace into the throng.

Angeline was quiet. Rachel felt sorry for her for the first time since meeting the woman. The constant sniping aimed at her was cruel and unnecessary. Even Marjorie, who could be happy to stir on occasions, was not stoking this fire. All in all, it was unpleasant to witness, but Rachel felt it important to remain, as things were being revealed that might throw some light on the investigation.

Had Cheryl been drinking? She seemed to have transformed from being an overanxious religious wallflower to a stubborn and unpleasant critic of her so-called friends. Blethyn gave as good as she received in an altogether more controlled manner, yet she was just as caustic as Cheryl. Angeline continued to be uncomfortable, as if she'd been found out, and Rachel suspected her crush on Mother Cross might be more than holy respect. Easter Balch had usurped her position as Mother's pet, but whether that would cause Angeline to murder her was a stretch.

The string quartet returned and the nuns got up quickly. "Goodnight, nice to see you again," said Letitia before following the others away from the atrium.

"Now that was enlightening. Altogether disagreeable, but enlightening," said Marjorie.

Rachel shook her head in disbelief. "I feel I need a wash. I don't think any of that lot will pass their training or take their vows."

"Apart from Letitia; she's a sweet girl. I wasn't quite sure what they were meaning with regards to Angeline, though. Were they suggesting—"

"She's gay? Yes, I think that's what they were implying. What a nasty pair of vipers. I liked Cheryl when we first met. She seemed more honest and unsure of the order for genuine reasons, but now she's downright nasty."

"She might just be fighting back, you know. I don't expect she's had an easy time with Blethyn and Angeline. It could be a case of the victim turning on the bullies. I feel she won with regards to Angeline, but I wonder if she won't regret saying those things later."

"You could be right there, Marjorie. She was the butt of their insults earlier in the cruise, wasn't she? Maybe if she's decided to leave, she feels able to say what she likes now without worrying about the consequences."

"I wonder if such behaviour is reported," said Marjorie.

"I doubt it, but it might come out in confessional. If they really are religious, there will be some guilt about how they behaved towards each other tonight."

"Perhaps they will be closer as a result. Maybe they're behaving like a family. Siblings do argue, after all."

Rachel shook her head again and widened her eyes. "I never argued with my brother like that."

"You're different, Rachel. For one thing, you're secure. Some of these girls come from vulnerable backgrounds and some have been spoilt, I'm certain of that."

"That's as maybe." Rachel smirked. "But on the positive side, I think I know now who killed Easter Balch."

She explained her theory to Marjorie. "I need to get into the Franks's room tomorrow. I think Gloria held the key to her daughter's murder, but she may not have realised it." Rachel was closing in on the killer; she just had to piece it all together and find the motive.

Chapter 29

Rachel jogged around the running track, enjoying the early morning sun and feeling satisfied that she was getting to the bottom of the two murders. It was going to be a scorcher today, so she had set the alarm to wake early and take some exercise before joining her party for a day out in St Thomas. It was the last land day and Sarah would be joining them, although Jason was working while Waverley took a rare day ashore.

Rachel had spoken to Carlos again last night before settling down. She knew that he questioned her sanity with regards to her murderous cruise habit, but the *Coral Queen* had a piece of her heart and there was no going back from that. The ship had provided her with so many memories, both good and bad. She had met Carlos and Lady Marjorie on her first voyage, so nothing could dissuade her from cruising despite the multiple murders she ended up investigating. Now it was time to conclude another investigation; she was certain that by the end of the day, there would be enough evidence to prompt a confession and provide motive.

She stopped in her tracks when she noticed a blue-habited figure sitting on a bench. Slowing down, she saw Angeline, crying.

"Are you all right?" she asked, stopping next to the lone nun.

The woman's lips trembled. "Not really."

"Would you like to talk about it?"

"It's true what they were implying last night, you know."

Rachel joined her on the bench. "It was a cruel way to point it out."

"The thing is, I'll never make a nun. How can I with this hanging over me?"

"Do you want to be a nun?"

"More than anything in the world."

"Then there's no reason why you can't be, if that's really what you want."

"But what about – you know?"

"I don't know much about your order, but does your sexuality matter? If you all take a vow of chastity, and mean it, it shouldn't matter which sex you are attracted to. The same temptation to break the vow exists for everyone, surely?"

"I hadn't thought of it like that. Blethyn will not let this go now she knows, though. She'll torment me forever."

"Then speak to your Mother Superior about it. Be honest with her and yourself. No-one can accuse you of anything if you don't hide it. I'm sure it won't be the first time she's spoken to someone in a similar position, and if you're serious about taking the vows, it's best to be open and honest. We all have things to hide – Blethyn too – so don't be afraid of human frailty. That's what my father always told me growing up."

Angeline looked up at Rachel, her dark brown eyes still glistening from the tears. "Thank you. I was rude to you when we first met. Blethyn said you and the old lady were busybodies and not to talk to you. I apologise."

"No need, and Blethyn's right in some ways. Marjorie and I are both inquisitive, particularly when it comes to things we don't understand like holy orders. Although my father's a vicar, I went to university and non-church schools, so your order is intriguing."

"You're lucky; I grew up in an orphanage. The kids there were supposed to be family, but it wasn't a happy time. The Order of the Blue Light is the only real family I've ever known. Mother Cross means everything to me; she is like a parent. The only thing is, I've wronged her deeply because I was disappointed."

"What do you mean?"

"I found out she'd had a baby before she became a nun. When she joined a Catholic convent before this order, she pretended to be a virgin. It haunted her, but she lied anyway. In those days, you had to be a virgin to join a Catholic convent; I'm not sure what the rules are now, but I think they might have relaxed them, as widows can be nuns if they want to. Our order doesn't have that rule."

"Did Mother Cross tell you all this?"

"No. I heard her praying and repenting of her sins. I was shocked and upset because I'd had her on a pedestal, so I ended up telling someone else."

431

Rachel already knew the answer, but asked anyway. "Who?"

"Easter – she's the nun that died in church on Sunday. She was evil, but I didn't know that at the time; I thought she was my friend. She was blackmailing Mother Cross about it, and Mother Cross then started spending loads of time with her before we came on this cruise. Easter told me she had discovered she and Mother Cross were related, but I didn't believe her. I was like the jealous sibling. One day I spied on them and realised that Easter was threatening to tell Sister Murdoch Mother Cross's secret. It was my fault. I don't think I can ever forgive myself."

It was just as Rachel had suspected, but she was certain that Easter had known about Mother Cross having given birth long before Angeline told her. She couldn't yet put the young woman's mind at rest, though, not while Angeline was still on the suspect list.

"Perhaps you should tell the Mother Superior."

"But, what if – I can't believe I'm saying this – what if Easter's death wasn't an accident? What if she was killed and Mother Cross did it? I caught her in Mother's room one day, looking under the mattress. She said she was making the bed, but I think she was looking for a diary or letters. Someone also rifled through my diary before we came on the cruise, and I'm certain it was her. She was evil, but if you repeat this conversation, I'll deny it. I won't bring any more harm to the Mother Superior."

"Do you think Mother Cross murdered Easter?"

"I don't know." Tears were falling once again down the confused woman's face.

"I've said enough; I'd like to be alone now."

"Okay," said Rachel, standing. "Try to enjoy St Thomas. I understand you're having a party tonight."

Angeline's face lit up. "Yes, although it's meant to be our big secret. It's Mother Cross's Golden Jubilee, so we're throwing a surprise dinner. The events manager has invited a whole crowd of Chinese businessmen, for some reason. I complained about it – Blethyn and I are on the committee for the party. It was kept quiet so Mother wouldn't find out. She thinks it's a business dinner held by our sponsor."

"I see." Rachel stroked her chin. "What is a Golden Jubilee, by the way?"

"It's a celebration for a nun reaching fifty years since taking their vows. All the more reason why I couldn't bear to see anything happen to our Mother Superior. It would ruin everything."

Rachel was no longer listening. The final pieces of the puzzle had come together for her. Now she just had to see Waverley.

"We need to gatecrash that party."

Rachel had caught Waverley just before he was due to leave ship for a day's snorkelling with his wife. Waverley heard her out and reluctantly agreed to do as she suggested; he would rather have dived in and made arrests immediately, but Rachel explained they needed to be patient and let the killer feel they were safe.

"I'll tell you more later, but I need to dash for a shower before meeting Marjorie for breakfast. Enjoy your snorkelling."

"How did you know about that? Don't tell me – Goodridge. There is no privacy on this ship, none at all."

As it turned out, Rachel almost regretted not going along with Waverley's suggestion, as she spent the day agitated and distracted during the tour. She had shared her conclusions with Marjorie over breakfast, but since then she had been stifled. Sarah had cancelled, feeling exhausted after another busy on call. Sometimes it was more important than anything for her to sleep and recharge.

"Do try to enjoy yourself, if only for your parents' sakes. Your mother thinks you're unwell," Marjorie whispered while they sat outside a café for lunch.

"Sorry. I'll be better this afternoon when we head up in the cable car. I'm actually looking forward to that."

"And I'm enjoying this beautiful island, so try to park your police brain for the time being, if you don't mind. You need to learn to compartmentalise, Rachel. Look at the beauty you're missing out on."

Marjorie was right; it was silly. Rachel was the one who had suggested waiting until this evening, and now she was ruining the day out. It was time to relax, especially as it was the last day ashore before two sea days followed by a long flight home. At least Carlos would be waiting for her. That thought brought a genuine smile to her face.

"Right, I'm back," she said as her parents joined them.

"We've just met a few of those young nuns," said Brendan.

"Really?" Rachel feigned disinterest.

"Yes, the bubbly one and the freckle-faced girl."

"Letitia and Cheryl. How did they seem?"

"Very happy, I think," said Susan. "They were on the way to rejoin a larger group before going out on a boat this afternoon."

"You'd think they would have had enough of being on the water, wouldn't you?" said Brendan. "I'm so looking forward to our Sky Ride this afternoon."

The Sky Ride was everything it was meant to be, with beautiful views over the harbour. There were two other cruise ships in port, but the *Coral Queen* was the biggest. They could see it during the ride. Afterwards, they split into pairs to do some duty-free shopping – something the island was famous for. Rachel bought her brother and Carlos a bottle of fine Scotch each, and Marjorie did the same for her son Jeremy. Rachel bought herself a pair of earrings. It was hard to buy anything else for Carlos, but she settled on a crystal decanter and glasses.

"Isn't that old-fashioned?" asked Marjorie.

"Yes, but he loves this sort of thing. Don't ask me why, but he does. I expect he'll put it in his office and fill the decanter with the Scotch for his clients."

"In that case, I'll be visiting his office." Marjorie's twinkling eyes made Rachel laugh for the first time that day.

Although the morning had dragged, Rachel had genuinely enjoyed the afternoon, and all too quickly it was time to meet up with her parents and head back to the ship for the final time before disembarkation. She took Marjorie's arm.

"Have you enjoyed your Caribbean adventure?"

"Oh yes, and don't worry, I've enjoyed it all the more for the murders. Although I would have preferred it if neither of the women had died."

"That's the problem. It's hard to have a murder without a body."

"What are you two talking about?" Rachel's mother appeared from a shop and the two women burst into fits of giggles.

"Marjorie, you're as bad as my daughter," Susan scolded.

"Time to head back, I think," said Brendan, catching up with them.

Rachel inhaled deeply.

"Yes, it's time."

Chapter 30

Once dinner was over, Rachel and Marjorie excused themselves from joining Rachel's parents at the theatre and headed towards the Jazz Bar where they had arranged to meet Sarah, Jason and Waverley.

The ship was buzzing with activity as passengers prepared for two days on board. Sea days allowed people to relax or party after the excursions on land, which was particularly welcome on a cruise like this one, Rachel thought, when they had stopped at five different islands. But although the excited atmosphere on board provided a welcome distraction, Rachel was feeling slightly nervous, anticipating what might go wrong tonight. There was always a nagging doubt she might have got parts of it completely wrong. Rachel also felt sorry for Connor, as Waverley had kept him under arrest so as not to alert the real killer, who would be more relaxed, thinking they had got away with their crimes.

Jason was already sitting in their regular booth, so they joined him.

"Are you ready?" he asked Rachel.

"Yes, I think so. Did you manage to get the information we needed from the FBI?"

"After some persuasion, the boss did it when he got back from shore leave. They wouldn't speak to me. He also spoke to Rodrigues, like you asked, and I checked the Franks's room. I think we have everything we need to close this out tonight. Here's the boss now." Jason handed Rachel a diary with some pages marked. Her jaw dropped open.

Waverley exuded health and happiness this evening. Marriage had done him a great favour; he was much less likely to get angry these days, although he could still be an idiot, as Marjorie frequently reminded her.

"Good evening, Chief," said Marjorie. "How was the snorkelling?"

Waverley huffed, just as he had done this morning when Rachel mentioned it. He hated having his personal life spread around ship.

"It was an experience."

Rachel shot Marjorie a look warning her not to pursue the matter. She didn't want the chief in a bad mood before they even got started.

"Shall we have a drink? Sarah's not here yet and we wouldn't want her to miss out."

"I don't know why we have to take a crowd of people in the first place. It's not professional," Waverley complained, but sat down anyway and ordered a brandy. A waiter had hurried towards the table after noticing the security chief was in the house.

"Sarah is part of the team and she's coming, Chief." Marjorie challenged him to respond with a glare. He got the message and turned to Rachel instead.

"You had better be right about all of this, Rachel. Otherwise I'm going to look a right fool."

Rachel nudged Marjorie not to say anything else. "I'm certain, but if you'd rather not go through with it, we can have another drink."

Waverley frowned. "Of course we're going through with it. Where is Sarah, Goodridge?" Waverley snapped.

So much for marriage suiting him, thought Rachel.

"I would have thought that was obvious, Chief," Marjorie was losing patience with Waverley's shortness. "She has a surgery and I expect she's dealing with a patient."

Waverley smiled sheepishly. "Sorry. I just want to get on, that's all."

"Don't we all?" retorted Marjorie.

"Here she is now, sir," said Jason.

Waverley jumped out of the chair, almost knocking the table over. "Right, let's get going then."

Sarah barely had time to say hello before she had to do an about turn and follow the chief as he marched them all towards one of the cocktail lounges. The signs outside it announced *"Private Party"*. The chief nodded to the crewman checking tickets and walked straight through, accompanied by Jason and the three women.

Abe Cooper was surrounded by a group of Chinese men and women dressed in tuxedoes and evening gowns. He glared when he saw Rachel and Marjorie.

"I feel positively underdressed," said Marjorie, chuckling. "But it's worth it to see that horrible man's face."

"What's the meaning of this?" The woman posing as Cooper's wife blocked the two women's path, allowing those in uniform, including Sarah, through. "This is a private party."

"They're with me," said Waverley, stopping just ahead of them and turning around. Other heads in the room turned towards them to see what the fuss was about. "Let's not cause a scene."

The woman checked Waverley's badge before giving a tight-lipped nod and standing aside. She followed them towards Cooper.

"Good evening. I'm Chief of Security Waverley, this is one of my officers, Jason Goodridge, ship's nurse, Officer Bradshaw, and these two women are Lady Marjorie Snellthorpe and Rachel Prince. Miss Prince I think you already know."

The Chinese contingent opened up the circle while Waverley fixed his eyes on Cooper, daring him to move.

"I don't think we've met. No, I would remember." Cooper attempted a smile, but it didn't work. The man was incapable of smiling. He turned to the Chinese guests. "Would you excuse us for a moment, please? The chief clearly has some security concerns."

"Indeed I do, but please stay." Waverley also addressed the Chinese businesspeople. "It will be good for you to know the kind of man you're dealing with." The chief smiled at the group, who remained where they stood. Esther Jordan tried to leave, but Jason escorted her back.

"Get on with it, Chief. As you can see, we are holding a private party and I have guests to entertain," growled Cooper, still playing it cool.

Waverley turned to Rachel. "Perhaps you'd like to explain why we're here, Miss Prince."

Rachel locked eyes with Cooper and detected a hint of fear. "Mr Cooper, Mrs Jordan," she glanced briefly towards his travel companion, "you have been on the radar of the FBI for misappropriation of funds from your billionaire sponsor for five years. So far, you have managed to keep your dealings hidden, particularly those relating to arms deals, drug trafficking and modern day slavery, but you made a mistake when you hired thugs to attack me in St Lucia. As you can see, I'm unharmed. The three men have since given full statements to the police."

Rachel prayed neither Waverley nor Marjorie would question this and was pleased when they didn't. She hoped rather than knew that this had happened.

"I don't know what you're talking about. Look, Chief, I don't know who this woman is, but she's clearly unhinged. This is some sort of mistake. I assure you my business dealings are legitimate."

A few of the Chinese contingent were looking uncomfortable now as more security and crew arrived, blocking the exit.

"We have managed to track every deal you've done on every island you've visited," Waverley said. "Unknown to you – and to us until earlier today – you've been under surveillance by the

FBI. I have spoken to the agent in charge of the operation and he believes they have enough evidence on you now to put you away for a long time. I think with their evidence and ours, your nefarious business dealings are over. Show him, Goodridge."

Jason held up a number of contracts taken from the safe in Cooper's room.

"You framed Mr Franks for hiring the thugs in St Lucia," Rachel continued. "You see, Mr Cooper, when someone is as nasty and arrogant as you are, they draw attention to themselves. I noticed you from the first sea day when you were too rude to draw a curtain to block out the sun from other passengers' eyes."

"Idiot," said Jordan. "Why couldn't you just blend in like you were told? All this because of a stupid curtain!"

"It's the little things," said Rachel. "As soon as those men tried to attack me, I knew there had to be someone who didn't want me prying into their business. Your links to Colin Bell have been your undoing."

Colin had been summoned and now joined them.

Rachel continued, "He inadvertently put you on to me by pointing me out and telling you I was a policewoman who had solved crimes on board the *Coral Queen* in the past. Without knowing it, Colin put me in danger."

"Is that right, Colin?" asked Jason.

Colin put his head down. "Yes, I'm sorry. I didn't realise."

"We have now traced all the transactions you've made on board ship, Mr Cooper, and logged your emails and telephone calls. The information gathered, along with that from the FBI, is enough for me to put you under arrest until we reach New York. Your billionaire sponsor has sent a message for you too. He says you're fired." Waverley summoned Ravanos. "Take this man to the brig."

"Have you released Connor?" asked Rachel.

"Yes," replied Waverley as the shocked Chinese contingent shuffled away from them while Ravanos led Cooper from the room. "You are under house arrest, Mrs Jordan. Unfortunately we won't have enough room for you in the brig when I've finished here, but rest assured, you're as guilty as your business partner. Please follow Officer Barrow over there."

"I didn't know about the men hired to attack you." Esther Jordan looked pleadingly at Rachel. "I'm not into violence."

"What do you think the people you do business with do, play tiddlywinks?" said Rachel coldly.

Jordan was led out, head down, as Mother Cross came over to join them.

"We just need to speak to a few of your nuns, Mother. Would you bring them over to a table, so we can let the party continue?" Waverley gave her the names and the Mother Superior's face reddened.

As the three women sat down, Mother Cross looking on anxiously, Rachel began speaking.

"As you know, on the day after we set sail, a sister from your order died suddenly. What three of you don't know is that her mother was also on board, and she was later murdered in order to frame her second husband for the first killing."

"You've lost me," snapped Sister Murdoch. "Are you saying that Sister Balch was murdered?"

"I am saying that, Sister. You yourself had motive to kill her, as you wanted to take over the order and drag it down into some sect where you could preach your own brand of hellfire and damnation. Easter asked too many questions; she was also a blackmailer."

Mother Cross audibly gasped.

"She threatened to tell the Mother Superior what you were up to unless you gave her money."

"What of it? It's not a crime to want to improve this outdated nonsense the Mother here advocates. I did not murder Easter Balch and I didn't know her mother was on board."

"No, but you had plenty of money, didn't you? You were employed by Abraham Cooper to carry money and documents through customs on his behalf. You passed on notes and meeting times, plus account numbers to people you met. Carla, the guide in San Juan, for one. You also recruited a few unwitting assistants, most likely telling them it was all for the cause you were brainwashing them into believing."

"Your room has been searched, Sister Murdoch. You will be escorted back there and placed under house arrest shortly," said Waverley, enjoying himself.

Rachel spoke next to Blethyn. "You turned a blind eye to what was going on under your nose. You knew about the blackmail, but are so blinded by the religion Sister Murdoch here peddles, you took her side. Whether you knew what else she was involved in will be up to the police to decide."

Blethyn crossed herself. "I will follow Sister Murdoch to the ends of the earth and the rest of you be damned!" she shouted. "But I did not kill anyone."

"No you didn't, because all the time, the killer was pretending to be a frightened little wallflower. Weren't you, Cheryl?"

Cheryl paled.

"Easter found out you had falsified your college qualifications and, being the blackmailer she was, turned her prying attention to you. Only this time, she had woken the dragon. You had already committed murder in your teens, hadn't you? Interestingly that's when you learned about digitalis poisoning from the foxglove plant. Your mother was a herbalist who dosed herself for a heart condition and taught you all about its poisonous properties. It appears your mother died suddenly of an *accidental* overdose of digitalis after the two of you argued.

"You left home shortly afterwards and went to college in New York, but there is no record of you ever attaining the qualifications you claimed you had to get in. Easter's uncle, who's an NYPD police officer, admitted his niece asked him to do a background check on you, which is when she found out about the false qualifications. What he didn't think was relevant at the time was how your mother died. Neither did he realise that Easter was a blackmailer who would not be satisfied until she dug out more dirt.

"You probably caught her going through your diary, a habit she appears to have had. You couldn't be certain how much of it she'd read, so you had to put a stop to her fishing and asking questions. You put your herbalist knowledge to good use again," Rachel raised the diary in the air, causing Cheryl to gasp, "first by killing Easter, and then by turning on her mother, Gloria Franks."

"You have no proof. I didn't know her mother; she told me they hadn't spoken in years."

"She pointed out her stepfather to you on the night of your onboard cocktail party, warning you to stay away from him. You were overheard by Colin Bell's wife, who was serving drinks, and were caught on CCTV."

"Would you check her pockets, please, Mother Cross?" asked Waverley.

The Mother Superior did as she was asked and drew out a bottle of digitalis tablets. She crossed herself and handed it to Waverley.

Rachel continued, "Connor Franks has identified you as speaking to his wife at Brimstone Hill Fortress, then the couple argued and she sent him away. You are a killer, Cheryl Sage. You got away with murdering your mother, but you won't get away with that any longer. Detective Rodrigues is looking forward to arresting you when we get to New York. All the evidence is in this diary, along with Easter's own diary retrieved from her mother's room today."

"I've been looking for that," Cheryl snapped.

"Easter had stored it in the purser's office, along with a bracelet given to her by her mother. The belongings had been delivered to Gloria's room while she was in St Kitts, otherwise the information in her daughter's diary would have saved her life. So why don't you tell us how you killed the two women?"

"Easter Balch was a no-good blackmailer, making everyone's life a misery. I had to share a room with her. I knew that Sister Faith was always leaving tablets lying around – she did it at the convent – so I took one of the bottles. It was easy to slip enough into Easter's breakfast before we went to church that morning, and then wait for it to take effect. She deserved to die. I was doing the world a favour, doing God's work."

Mother Cross crossed herself again.

"What about her mother?" asked Rachel. "Why did you want to kill her?"

"The opportunity presented itself when we were up the hill. I heard Mother Cross telling one of the other older nuns – not you, Sister Murdoch, she didn't trust you – that a policewoman might be joining us to investigate Easter's death. I snuck into her room when she went for prayers – the lock was sticking on her door, and if it wasn't pulled closed properly, it was easy to get in – and I saw your name scribbled on a pad, but didn't know who you were until we met at our art class. I could tell by looking at you that you were watching us, you and the old girl."

Marjorie huffed.

"I decided it would be better to have the finger pointing elsewhere, and as I knew Easter didn't like her stepfather, he seemed the ideal candidate. I also knew that Easter kept a diary and it might find its way to her mother. I told her that Easter had given me a message for her before she died; she lapped it up."

"And when you drew her away, you injected her with digitalis, dissolved in water. Where did you get the syringe and needle?"

"Sister Cook is diabetic. I grabbed one of hers in case I needed it to kill Easter, but if she ate the digitalis, it would be less obvious that it might be murder."

More sisters had gathered around by now, and they crossed themselves in unison. Waverley coughed.

"Cheryl Sage, you are under arrest for the murder of Easter Balch and for the murder of Gloria Franks. You will be locked in the brig until we reach New York – we have kept enough room aside for a cold-blooded killer – when you will be handed over to the port authorities. I think you'll find that the death of your mother has also been reinvestigated."

Cheryl glared towards Waverley, and then at Rachel.

"I should have dealt with you as well, but don't worry; when I get out, I'm coming for you." She cackled loudly.

"Join the queue," said Rachel, holding her gaze.

Waverley interrupted. "Sister Murdoch, you are under arrest for money laundering and smuggling. Officer Barrow will escort you back to your room now she has returned. Goodridge, you can take Sage away."

Blethyn made the wise choice to leave the company and the party. The other nuns were encouraged to return to their tables. Mother Cross looked at Waverley and the others.

"Thank you for not revealing my secret or the subsequent blackmail. It's high time I confessed anyway. I'll do so on our return."

"It wasn't relevant to the murders," said Rachel.

"I hope the church authorities take into account your years of dedication and service," said Marjorie.

Mother Cross held her crucifix. "Some Golden Jubilee. At least justice will be done."

"At last. Enjoy your party," said Waverley.

The group left the cocktail lounge and Waverley excused himself to fill out his records.

"You've done it again, Rachel Prince," said Sarah. "And you, Marjorie."

"Hmph," said Marjorie. "Nasty business. At least the order turned out to be relatively normal, give or take a murderer, a smuggling racket and a planned coup."

The three women laughed.

"And the Armageddon thing turned out to be delusions after all," added Sarah.

"Yes. Plus you have to admit that Waverley was right about one thing," said Rachel.

"What?"

"You were not followed back to your room that night. Blethyn must have got off on deck seven and the man on deck fifteen was a drunk after all."

"Well, I suppose the man has to get some things right, but it's a good thing he's always got Rachel around when it comes to solving murders."

Marjorie chuckled. The three women joined arms.

"How about a drink in the Jazz Bar?" suggested Sarah.

"Ooh, now that sounds just the ticket," said Marjorie. "Will you be telling your parents about this, Rachel?"

"Not likely! I'll let Waverley take the credit."

"Hmph!"

The trio giggled as they walked happily towards their favourite bar.

THE END

Author's Note

Thank you for reading *Murderous Cruise Habit*, the sixth book in the Rachel Prince Mystery series. If you have enjoyed it, please leave an honest review on Amazon and/or any other platform you may use. I love receiving feedback from readers and can assure you that I read every review.

Keep an eye out for Book 7. *Honeymoon Cruise Murder* will be released in autumn 2020.

Keep in touch:

Sign up for my no-spam newsletter at:
https://www.dawnbrookespublishing.com

Follow me on Facebook:
https://www.facebook.com/dawnbrookespublishing/

Follow me on Twitter:
@dawnbrookes1

Follow me on Pinterest:
https://www.pinterest.co.uk/dawnbrookespublishing

Acknowledgements

Thank you to my editor Alison Jack, as always, for her kind comments about the book and for suggestions, corrections and amendments that make it a more polished read. Thanks to Alex Davis for the final proofread, corrections and suggestions.

Thanks to my beta readers for comments and suggestions, and for their time given to reading the early drafts.

Thanks to my immediate circle of friends who are so patient with me when I'm absorbed in my fictional world and for your continued support in all my endeavours.

I have to say thank you to my cruise loving friends for joining me on some of the most precious experiences of my life

and to the cruise lines for making every
holiday a special one.

About the Author

Dawn Brookes is author of the *Rachel Prince Mystery* series, combining a unique blend of murder, cruising and medicine with a touch of romance.

Dawn has a 39-year nursing pedigree and takes regular cruise holidays, which she says are for research purposes! She brings these passions together with a Christian background and a love of clean crime to her writing.

The surname of her protagonist is in honour of her childhood dog, Prince, who used to put his head on her knee while she lost herself in books.

Bestselling author of *Hurry up Nurse: memoirs of nurse training in the 1970s* and *Hurry up Nurse 2: London calling,*

Dawn worked as a hospital nurse, midwife, district nurse and community matron across her career. Before turning her hand to writing for a living, she had multiple articles published in professional journals and coedited a nursing textbook.

She grew up in Leicester, later moved to London and Berkshire, but now lives in Derbyshire. Dawn holds a Bachelor's degree with Honours and a Master's degree in education. Writing across genres, she also writes for children. Dawn has a passion for nature and loves animals, especially dogs. Animals will continue to feature in her children's books as she believes caring for animals and nature helps children to become kinder human beings.

Books by Dawn Brookes

Rachel Prince Mysteries
A Cruise to Murder
Deadly Cruise
Killer Cruise
Dying to Cruise
A Christmas Cruise Murder
Murderous Cruise Habit

Memoirs
Hurry up Nurse: memoirs of nurse training in the 1970s
Hurry up Nurse 2: London calling
Hurry up Nurse 3: More adventures in the life of a student nurse

Coming Soon 2020
Book 7 in the Rachel Prince Mystery series
Honeymoon Cruise Murder

Look out for a New Crime Novel Series
in 2020 featuring Carlos Jacobi, PI
Body in the Woods

Picture Books for Children

Ava & Oliver's Bonfire Night Adventure
Ava & Oliver's Christmas Nativity
Adventure
Danny the Caterpillar
Gerry the One-Eared Cat
Suki Seal and the Plastic Ring

Made in the USA
Middletown, DE
06 September 2021